for fan

CW00417320

Copy right @ 2021 Robert Price
All rights reserved

The characters and events portrayed in this book are
fictitious. Any similarity to real persons, living or dead,
is coincidental and not intended by the author.

No part of this book may be reproduced, or stored in a
retrieval system, or transmitted in any form or by any
means, electronic, mechanical, photocopying, recording,
or otherwise, without express written permission of the
publisher.

ISBN-13: 9798744032982
ISBN-10: 1477123456

Cover design by: Art Painter
Library of Congress Control Number: 2018675309
Printed in the United States of America

Introduction

Prime Minister Rupert Streaker is chancing his arm with his own party being popular with the general public.

A radical strategy to enhance his reputation in order to receive public acknowledgement and thereby, the erection of a personal statue outside the new Parliament buildings in Blackburn. An ambition brought with him from childhood. However, internal rivals are furious over his attempts to maintain honesty and cost savings in relation to the move. Traditional vested interests are at stake raising the temperatures of those ordinarily expected to support him. Losing out not something they had signed up to by electing him. As tribal warfare breaks out within his own party those on the opposite benches can only spectate uncertain whether   or   not   to   cheer.

CHAPTER ONE

The separation between categorized predator and someone accepting an open sexual invitation can be slim, especially if you happen to be Prime Minister. That was the dilemma confronting Rupert Streaker as he observed Mata Harris bending stretching and kneeling while reorganising the books on the shelves beside his desk. For more than a half hour his attention which should have been focused on the latest news about the Relocation Project of Parliament to Blackburn had been redirected to the ripe fulsome breasts and bulbous buttocks that strained her short skirt. Added to them a dark pair of tights over shapely legs and plump thighs ending at black stilettos provided an image someone with the libido of a jack rabbit couldn't ignore.

The more he watched the more he was certain that she was up for sexual shenanigans. However, the phrase 'don't shit where you eat' repeatedly flashed through his mind. Harris was a temp sent over by the Home Office to stand in for his personal secretary Bernice Walters who was currently on leave. With just one more day left before Walters return an inner argument raged whether he should bite the bullet just to see if his instincts were correct. As she knelt by the shelf buttocks high head low scanning the titles he rose from behind the desk and moved unflinchingly towards her delectable rear hands poised. Just inches away the office door crashed open and Jonathon Bandip his personal aide appeared. Anxious and breathless.

"I need to speak to you Rupert!"

"What now?" He snapped unhappily. About to make first contact with the rounded posterior.

"It's urgent," he insisted.

Streaker pulled his hands away slipping them behind his back as he returned to his desk. "Mata give us a minute will you."

She rose quickly and left them the door closing behind her.

"This better be good Jonathon," he grumbled with the image of Harris's rear end taunting him.

"Harris is a plant."

"For whom the Chinese, Russians, North Korea?"

"Jessica."

He dropped back on the seat with a heavy thud, "Blasted woman doesn't trust me. Thinks I'd grab the first attractive female that makes herself available!"

"Did you?" Bandip asked uncertainly.

"Nearly, but no I didn't. How do you know she's a plant?"

"My contact at the Home Office. Apparently Mata Harris is regularly used by the wives of senior civil servants to test their fidelity."

He released a heavy sigh, "Bloody Hell! Trying to have a bit of fun these days is getting harder and harder. There was a time when the Prime Minister could whip a wench's skirts up give her a good rogering and she'd be grateful. And they call this progress."

In 1895 perhaps Bandip thought but the world has thankfully moved on. "Well, no harm done. Looks like we avoided another silver bullet."

Streaker frowned angrily, "I'm going to have a word with Jessica. I can't live with the woman checking my behaviour with every pretty girl who steps in front of me. It's just not fair."

"If you mention Harris you'll be revealing our contact at the Home Office. If she thinks you knew why Harris was here she might try again."

"Damn!" He grunted annoyed. "But I can't let her get away with it."

"She hasn't," he reminded him. "Fact is you're the one who had the narrow escape. If you'd touched Harris Jessica would probably be here now and your marriage might well be over."

"It would be the sixth. God I'm lousy at marriage."

"Then why do you do it?" Bandip asked genuinely curious.

He shook his head. "It seems the right thing to do at the time. Besides the job likes its leaders to appear as family men."

"A heavy price to pay if you're someone who can't be satisfied with one woman," He said. Hiding that he felt more sympathy for Streaker's wife and children. Why she took the risk marrying him a mystery. His reputation and infidelities were common knowledge in every circle. Perhaps, he wondered, it was because she thought she could change him? He had heard that argument often enough. Except Streaker had been born into a wealthy family that bred superiority. Spoiled as part of an elite group who considered themselves above everyone else. Inhibitions were muted as were morals. She must have been aware what she was getting herself into. Streaker himself had told him that her family had been against the marriage. Possibly defying them another reason why she had gone ahead with it. Or perhaps it simply highlighted yet again that *love is blind*. "I'll get rid of Harris immediately."

"You will?" Streaker appeared disappointed

"She's far too close to your tastes Rupert. We can't risk it. You might be tempted to reach out if she chooses to place any of her parts at your disposal. Another scandal at this time would scupper you."

"I suppose you're right," he replied glumly.

CHAPTER TWO

Relocating Parliament to Blackburn was an unpopular move among many ministers who saw it as a leaving the prestige of the capital and therefore downgrading their lofty positions in the capital. Additionally, it was an inconvenience and unnecessary upheaval to their way of life. London with its 8 million plus population remained the main attraction for tourism and trade. Businesses flocked there to negotiate deals with government and the financial houses. The financial quarter remained fixed in Canary Wharf and Threadneedle Street home of the Bank of England. However, Prime Minister Rupert Streaker had used public opinion to overwhelm all arguments against the relocation north to Blackburn. Demanding that ministers acknowledge the genuine distrust of millions outside the M25 London ring suspicious that Westminster barely recognized their existence. A majority of the people wanted Parliament situated more centrally in the country and Blackburn was ideally placed.

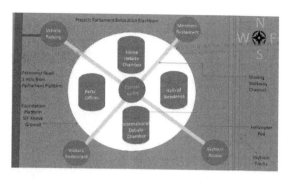

Project: Parliament Relocation Blackburn

By 2022 construction had already begun at the site outside the city. In a picturesque part of Green belt within the Witton Country Park. A 480-acre natural mix of woodland and park land west of Blackburn. A landscape of emerald, green from the sky boxed by brown hedges and roads. Today much of the lush green had disappeared replaced by the dark brown grey of construction. The site had been contested by both environmentalists and local people particularly as the new Parliament would gobble up more than 200 acres of natural beauty. However, complaints were drowned out by a powerful northern lobby intent on ensuring that Parliament finally be centred in the UK and, thereby provide citizens north of the M25 with some comfort that London no longer cornered the primary attention of Westminster. Moving ministers away from their London homes a major step in ensuring their acknowledgement that the new area in which they resided required improved infrastructure and support. Something they had repeatedly asked and promised for more than a decade.

Confirmation that the new relocated Parliament was intended to show that the political elite took seriously the need to address public concerns in the north over being forgotten. It arrived in the form of the Queen's new formal residence moving from Buckingham Palace to Lancaster Castle. A medieval construction of tall turrets and high stone walls installed in Lancashire during the eleventh century. A formidable war experienced stronghold that defended against Scottish invasion and centuries later supported the Monarchy during the English Civil War. However, it is possibly remembered more for having served as a prison until 2011. Over the centuries it was used to hold the Pendle Witches in the early 17th century. Doing such a good job that political prisoners were also sent to it including Quakers who were considered politically dangerous at the time. Additionally, before 1800 those sentenced to death were taken to Lancaster Moor to be hanged. With such a turbulent history one might have been forgiven thinking the castle haunted and, if the Queen had her doubts about her new residence, she remained tight lipped as did her family.

However, Streaker was not unaware of the potential goodwill the Royals might heap on him if presented with accommodation that far exceeded expectations. Nor that for the people outside of London having the Queen closer meant far more than parliament ever could. For those reasons he included in the Castle refurbishment a new stable for her carriage and horses, kennels for her dogs together with an onsite medical team fully equipped to deal with anything from a stubbed toe to heart surgery. No expense spared. The result came days later after they had discussed the move. Arriving in a letter stating her delight at the idea of leaving Buckingham Palace to live in the countryside. Something she admitted that she wished had been done sooner. Thanking and assuring him of her support for the move. It was icing on a cake. Melody to his ears. Something no one in the Party could ignore. A seal of approval like no other.

However, the Prime Minister had been under serious criticism over his failure to inform the public that contaminated imported American brewery equipment was responsible for spreading COVID. Contact between the equipment and alcohol triggering the passive virus contained in metal piping. Rex Pounding, leader of the opposition had exposed Streaker's failure and repeatedly attacked him over it. Maintaining a consistent reference to his failure for the last twelve months. However, the British political system reaches a point after which there is no accountability. None. Zilch. Streaker had passed that point months ago and avoided a civil war within his own Party beating off challenges for his job by using public popularity for his major changes including the relocation of Parliament. Feeling fireproof he strode onwards more determined to achieve his goal of a personal statue erected outside the new Parliament building as an expression by the people that he was the best P.M. ever.

In a mobile office at the new parliament construction site away from Westminster and its political disruption. Head of the Parliament Project Bernard Allfores, stared down at architectural plans relating to the foundations currently being laid. Allfores had been promoted to head the project after his wife and Streaker were exposed as having had an affair during his days at university. An ensuing coverup extricated the Prime Minister from responsibility diverting attention away from him at an unknown other. While Kate Allfores was sacrificed due to a tattoo of Lassie the wonder dog on her buttocks. Twenty years later the tattoo remained where most of the UK had seen it on a photograph circulated across social media and every national newspaper. Once in the clear Streaker had had Kate reassigned to a nuclear bunker project deep underground and out of sight. However, she had chosen to tell her husband the truth. Hence, they were currently estranged. Not that Bernard had allowed it to end there. He approached Streaker with demands for his silence, one being a promotion to a grade within the Civil Service more associated with people from families with status. Giving Streaker no wriggle room. Coincidentally, Allfores timing could not have been better as the P.M. and Jonathon Bandip his personal fixer had come up with the parliament relocation project as a way of diverting public attention away from pressing issues such as increasing numbers of homeless and poverty among children. The public usually easy to distract went along with the importance of relocating Parliament to a more central part of the UK. Those in the north were expectedly ecstatic while members of the 'old guard' in the Tory party publicly argued and complained which only appeared to make public support for the move stronger. No one liked whingers especially toffee-nosed ones.

For Allfores it was the opportunity he had dreamt about. Coming from what his peers considered as humble origins with academic qualifications that were competitive but a family less so. It was an opportunity he could never have gotten any other way and he was going to make the most of it. As for his wife he no longer knew how he felt about her even after more than twelve months. The fact that she had allowed her affair to continue with Streaker until very recently made doubting her ability to remain loyal doubtful. If he couldn't trust her, even though he still loved her, he couldn't live wondering whether she was meeting someone else when late home. He deserved better. Their marriage felt a sham. Almost a waste of both their times. More than ten years. These days he kept busy by focusing on work rather than emotional issues. Infinitely easier to live with.

The plans and images laid out before him intended as a demonstration of how the use of modern technology allowed both Parliamentary Houses to appear as the most modern state-of-the-art structures in the entire country perhaps even Europe. Pushing the boundaries of architectural design and recent energy efficiency advances they were meant to raise expectations of a new wave of radical building design made necessary by climate change as well as terrorist activity. The House of Commons remained the first House while the Lords became The Second Chamber.

The main buildings together with their separate arteries were hamlets. An intention to reflect their independence from one another. Looking down at the plans he felt a surge of pride invade his emotions at being the individual chosen to lead the project no matter how his appointment came about. He would prove once and for all that he was up-to-the-job as well as any of his wealthy contemporaries.

From above the buildings appeared crown-like in the way they stretched out from two mammoth central discussion chambers using six corridor channels that connected to ringed perimeter buildings comprising four level square modules. The web of tentacled corridors criss-crossing one another for quick access to the administrative and accommodation areas contained within each module. Their stainless-steel outer casing resistant to erosion while their arched roofs comprised Solar Panels beneath hardened glass.

However, at ground level the buildings took on a different appearance. Standing twenty feet above ground a measure against flooding they dwarfed the natural tree filled landscape surrounding them. Atop platforms disguised as part of their structure their true capabilities remaining unrecognized. In reality each module level was a separate watertight entity that could be airlifted and flown to a safe haven should a threat ever make it necessary. Alternatively, they could be lowered onto water and power themselves to nearby safe harbours.

If faced with danger the corridors automatically disengaged to allow modules freedom of movement. After that they lifted up raising themselves vertically against the central chamber until they appeared like tall spires. Their secondary function to act as life pods to any overspill of people in either of the central chambers which were weight limited to one hundred. Once boarding was completed the life pods were disengaged and left either on the ground or water with a rescue beacon signalling their location. On land or sea life pods were mobile operated by a crew of three. Allowing Government to continue governing the intention behind the survival features adopted by the building designers.

Beneath both structures tarmac had been laid. Flat, without the hint of a ripple or bump. Space for fifty vehicles each. The only type of vehicle allowed on the Parliamentary Estate. Hydrogen four-seater chariots. Their purpose to transport ministers between the main buildings and other areas of the estate including a helicopter landing area close to its perimeter.

Additionally, one of the preconditions was a need for residences to house foreign ambassadors. Seen as a priority over housing UK ministers the latter were dealt with tactfully, taking care not to upset the already agitated Tories in particular who opposed the relocation. A level within each module complex was appointed Ambassadorial Suites and afforded every luxury. Additionally, all Commonwealth countries of which there remain fifty-four were provided permanent areas as were the Americans.

The six hundred and fifty House of Commons M.P.s except Cabinet members were built a new accommodation complex a short distance outside the Parliamentary Estate. The MP Residential Complex was a mini-town complex that also included homes for the families of the Second Chamber Representatives (SCR). However, for security reasons it was deemed necessary that a mini mall be included to negate the need for families to venture outside a wired perimeter guarded by private security. In all the Complex accommodated more than six thousand people with two thousand employed in the mall and for maintenance. Additionally, each family was provided a free electric chariot for transport for the Complex and Parliamentary Estate.

Arguments erupted in the local area over the loss of considerable Green belt and the public cost of building MP accommodation. However, in defence the Government pointed out the creation of two thousand jobs in an area with high unemployment. In addition, the creation within the Parliamentary Estate of a further two thousand jobs and a potential for another thousand. The politicians would argue for months but in the end the Prime Minister would get his way. Streaker was no fool he knew how to work a crowd. The public were putty in his hands provided he gave them jobs and did things that appeared for the good of all four countries in the Kingdom.

Allfores was happy to be out of it. He detested politics and politicians no one more than Rupert Streaker who destroyed his marriage. The thought of him with his wife Kate still too raw to contemplate. It wasn't easy be a cuckold husband. Always wondering what people were saying behind your back. Believing every snigger was aimed at you. It was all too easy to allow paranoia to take hold. Too easy to hate the person who put you on the spot. He sighed to himself. Hating Kate, a pointless exercise. Their affair happened. Hanging on to the anger he felt when first discovering the truth wouldn't change anything. It only acted to cripple him. To divert him from what he needed to do. To leave his past behind. To begin afresh with new hopes on the horizon. That's what he was doing. Reaching for the stars. Motivated to show everyone that he was as good as any and better than most.

He hadn't spoken to Streaker since accepting the role of Project Leader almost two years ago. Their relationship too tenuous to test either his patience or inner rage. Clearly, Streaker appreciated his feelings and used Jonathon Bandip as their personal go-between. Bandip the smoothest operator he had ever encountered. An individual with an answer for everything and anything. A friend of Streaker's from his days at university. The Prime Minister liked to surround himself with friends from his youth. It was a club of sorts. Perhaps they had always known they were destined to become the most powerful individuals in the country? How that was possible beyond him yet there they were.

The minister he had seen more than any other was Martin Probe Secretary of State for Housing. Probe appeared to have the task of monitoring every move he made and quickly became a regular visitor to the mobile office. It may have been that he had been expected to fail early on. He did not doubt it was what many wanted if for no other reason than to use contractors who charged the earth and saw that ministers received a pay-out for the privilege. Allfores had been determined from the outset to cut costs without cutting quality and fought like a lion to secure contractors outside the 'old boys' network. Using the affair between his wife and Streakers as leverage whenever needed. So far, Bandip had acquiesced after consultation with the Prime Minister. Saving millions of pounds by doing so while attracting genuine hatred from Probe and many others in the Party.

After a time learning the rules of the game, he was playing together with its threshold limits lessened the impact of having a target on his back.

Never one to flaunt power he remained discrete and focused on the project. It proved a winning combination provided Streaker remained in the power seat. Oddly, he came to realize just how useful having the Prime Minister onside proved to be. Growing anxious when the possibility of him being dethroned suddenly appeared likely. Especially when the American contamination of the breweries shattered the news. Rex Pounding, leader of the opposition had taken great pains going into detail over the issue in a televised parliamentary session of Prime Minister's Questions. It had all looked absolutely hopeless for Streaker. Yet somehow, he survived. What shocked Allfores most was his own relief that he had done so. The man he hated most needed to remain in place for him to complete the project and receive all the applause he was warranted. It made him realize that without Streaker everything good that had happened with his career would have remained a dream. Always out of reach. He found it emotionally confusing.

No more so than when he had to deal with his wife who was leading the Old Buildings Project back in Westminster. Their conversations initially artificial. Formal. Some months passed before their interaction was able to shelve the complexities of their situation. Only happening because they both wanted it. Kate Allfores was as career minded as her husband and as determined to succeed as he perhaps because she felt that she had even more to prove? She had heard the term slut several times while in her new role, sometimes the word mentioned loudly purposely. It had been her who had made the call for a ceasefire at work. Her who suggested how they proceed and spoke about of what they both had to lose if either of them failed. He admired her for that. But did not forgive her. Maybe he never would?

The door to the mobile office opened. The work of construction suddenly loud making him look up from the desk. Probe stepped inside closing the door behind him. Shutting out the unwanted sounds. "Morning Bernard."

"I didn't expect to see you today," he said glumly. His wife still on his mind.

"Well don't sound so cheerful about it," Probe said.

He apologised, "Sorry, I was distracted. What brings up here today?"

"I've a new contractor to help with the cabling that I'd like you to consider," Probe had learned not to assume Allfores would automatically accept any contractor. Learning that nothing was a 'given' taking time. He was still learning as were his peers back in Westminster.

"I haven't asked for any additional contractors?" Allfores pointed out.

Probe sucked in a deep breath as if knowing this would be difficult. "Look, Bernard the government needs to be seen helping companies maintain business. It's the only way the economy can survive. You know it's been an uphill struggle to reach this point doing as well as we have."

Some doing better than others he thought. "What's the name of this company you're trying to keep afloat?"

"Beanno."

"That's huge," he replied already irritated. The number of times Probe had attempted to do a favour for a friend lost in treble digits. How much he would expect as a payoff reflected by the effort he put into pushing Allfores to accept. "A cabling job is hardly going to impact on the billions they collect every year. I thought the idea was to keep companies afloat not build their wealth for them?"

"Try not to be awkward Bernard. Just this once."

"We don't need them Martin and I'm not paying for anything that's not needed this project is costing enough as it is. As Project Manager I have the final say and you should know by now that parasites aren't wanted."

"I knew you'd be like this, but I thought I'd try. One day you won't have the ear of the PM and when that happens, you'll be history."

"Until that day comes don't bother me with pleas for your rich mates!"

Probe turned away without speaking and stormed out. The door hanging open behind him. The sound of construction work again louder. Allfores gently closed the door with a sigh. The threat of his removal always present. A constant reminder of the part played by Streaker. Like him or loathe him he was a necessary evil.

It was late afternoon when he received a call from Bernice Walters Streaker's personal secretary. An anomaly that he couldn't fathom. In her early fifties a recognized long-term supporter of the Party hence her position at Number 10. Yet, as a reflection of the 'Old Guard' her appearance alongside Streaker's fresh approach to government appeared at odds. However, it must have been his decision that she remain where she had been for more than a decade. Perhaps she, like Allfores, possessed leverage?

"Hello Bernice, what can I do for you?"

"The PM wanted me to check that your morning meeting with the Housing Minister didn't cause you too many problems."

"He knows about it," he said sounding surprised. "Of course, he does," an image of Probe complaining to other ministers over his unwillingness to allow '*friendly companies*' to syphon off public money would quickly circulate. He should have expected as much. "You can tell him the only one suffering is the Minister. My stance on personally selecting companies to this project hasn't changed. No matter who threatens me."

"I see," she said. Tone neutral.

"As long as I have his support," he added.

A pause from her end suggested she was taking a moment to give him a considered reply. "He does support you Bernard. Trust me on that."

He thought he detected a hint of sympathy in her tone, "That's gratifying to hear Bernice."

"People outside the Westminster bubble have begun to notice what you're doing. People who appreciate just how difficult an undertaking it is for you."

It was his turn to pause. Her remark rich with interpretations that he had small chance of fully understanding. She would know it. Perhaps offering him an *olive leaf*? He sighed. Politics. Games people played at the expense of others. He detested it all. Not a politician himself the devious strategies always contained more traps than a yellow brick road. His wary response necessary, "The media still complain about the costs though."

"Then it's a good job you didn't open the gate for the big sharks," she said. "Personally, I'm proud of what you've achieved."

When a conversation reaches a point that leaves one side completely at a loss it's time to quit. "Thank you, Bernice. You can tell the PM that it's business as usual."

"I will," she replied and ended the call.

He sat back in the chair reeling from the implications that Walters had placed in his mind. No one ever spoke about their personal view in such contested situations. She was meant to remain neutral. Of course, it might have been a trick. Streaker playing games. Except he had no reason to do so.

CHAPTER THREE

Feathered Friends

That evening Streaker was alone reading The Times in the private residence at Number 10. The residence of the Prime Minister of the United Kingdom. Also, the headquarters of government. Built over 300 years ago these days it contained about 100 rooms with more than one hundred staff. Originally comprising three houses the first Prime Minister Sir Robert Walpole was offered the properties by King George II in 1732. He accepted the gift with the proviso it was given to the First Lord of the Treasury and not to him personally. Walpole enlisted the services of William Kent to join the three properties and today it is the larger property known as Number 10.

In the far corner two African Grey parrots stood on separate perches watching him. Animals birds included rely on instinct when faced by a predator and tend to fall silent as a way of avoiding detection. The fact that both parrots were completely still and silent testimony to their feelings regarding Streaker. Only when he was joined by his wife Jessica, their owner, did they exit their traumatised state.

"The kids are in bed and I need a glass of wine," she said entering the room. "Would you like one?"

He looked up from the paper, smiled and shook his head. "I've something stronger already darling."

She moved across to a drinks tray and reached for a 2017 Chateau Lynch-Bages. A bottle almost empty from the previous evening. What remained filled half a glass. Her eyes closed as she sipped the red medium bodied wine. Her French favourite.

"You should drink less European wines darling," he said watching her. "People notice what we buy and no doubt it'll end up in the news. Since we're out of the EU I'd like you to consider alternatives."

"I happen to like French wines Rupert. Does it really matter that they're French?"

"At a hundred and forty-five pounds a bottle someone is bound to complain. It is public money you're spending after all and they don't like to see us financially supporting the French instead of our own."

She came across and plonked down next to him on the sofa, "You must sometimes ask yourself whether all this nonsense is worth it."

"What do you mean?"

"I mean we have to be careful not to buy foreign produce in case we upset one in every hundred members of the public. It's insane you know. Why can't we just be who we are."

"Because we have responsibilities that we cannot ignore," he replied. Knowing that she understood made their conversation irritating for him, but he remained calm and showed none of the signs that might give away what he was really thinking.

"They never stopped you before," she said turning closer to him. "What's changed. I know something has because you've been different for quite a while?"

"More people than ever want me to fail."

"You mean more people from your Party," she replied qualifying his statement. "It has something to do with the relocation of Parliament doesn't it?"

"It's Bernard Allfores," he replied seriously. "He's too damn honest!"

She shrugged, "Replace him."

"He's doing too good a job. The public like what they're hearing about him. Saving public money at the expense of the big construction companies. Helping the smaller companies by bringing them onboard the project instead."

"You must have chosen him for a reason," she asked interest growing. She had always suspected it had something to do with his wife Kate and the alleged affair between Streaker and her even though her husband had empathically denied it. It seemed possible the cracks in his defence were beginning to reveal themselves with Bernard Allfores making a nuisance. "Why did you promote him to Project Leader?"

"I told you he's the right man for the job. I just didn't imagine he was so right. The papers are full of his efforts to stamp out the use of our usual big contractors in favour of smaller ones."

"You mean he's honest," she said gauging his reaction. "Maybe it's a good thing. The public are tired of hearing about corruption in government. Under your authority he's changing that. He's a reflection of you."

"Trouble is too many construction investors feel they're losing out. They're a powerful bunch."

"Stick with Allfores," she said dismissing his reticence. "You have a dream. The only way you might reach it could be by backing honesty over greed. There are other major projects in play, just ensure the concerned companies are afforded preferential treatment with them."

He smiled, "You always have the answer." It was a reason he loved her. Astute enough to quickly appraise a situation and assess the necessities to overcome obstacles. She was a canny chess player, something learnt from her father. Seeing three or four moves ahead to decide on the best strategy.

"You're just too close to the problem but I do need something from you."

"What's that?"

"Tell me that you didn't shag Kate Allfores either at university or later?"

"How many times do I need to tell you that before you believe me?"

"As many times as I ask," she said.

"I've never shagged Kate Allfores. There is that good enough?"

"Shag! Shag!" Pecker one of the parrots chirped.

He sighed, "One of these days that bird is going to give itself a heart attack."

"He enjoys sex as much as you," she kissed him. "Besides, they have long lives. Some live as long as seventy or eighty. I'm sure I'll be able to see to it that he outlives us."

Wonderful. He thought. The notion of being outlived by a parrot that would likely receive accolades over being their pet likely meant a statue of the bird being made. The awful thought suddenly crossed his mind perhaps of his own statue and the possibility of a parrot on each shoulder included! Nothing could be worse he thought. He would look like a two-legged version of Long John Silver! If all the birds ever said was shag it would be another slur on his memory. Immortalized by shag shrieking parrots! He pushed the awful thought away and forced a smile, "Maybe it's time for bed?"

"Shag! Shag! The bird repeated behind them.

"At least he has the right idea," she laughed.

CHAPTER FOUR

The Reporter

Being a reporter in the twenty first century was not easy. Boris Daley had enough years behind him to know better times. Not that it had ever proven easy to find a scoop, but today people were more discriminating and highly suspicious. Far less willing to divulge anything that might incriminate bad people than might ordinarily be expected. Honest folk found it easier to keep quiet than speak out. It was how those with bad intentions flourished. Abusing their positions within government to pursue their own interests. The public were shocked by the MP expenses scandal back in 2008, while only a handful were charged and sent to prison. The remainder eluding what the ordinary man in the street could never have done. It was a sign of the times. A demonstration of the inequality bubbling just below the surface.

The expenses scandal should have been a warning flag to the public. However, people were too busy surviving day-to-day to pass more than glancing attention. Lofty affairs of State not something they could add to their busy agendas. Besides, assurances by government, that is those involved and with reason to carefully extricate themselves and colleagues from allegations of wrongdoing were the same ones relied upon to do what was right for the country. Like that was ever going to happen.

Few voiced concern after the leadership on either side of the House remained unchanged. While some asked for a fresh general election with new candidates untainted by the embarrassing scandal. They were mostly ignored their voices lost among others with more to lose. However, the government and opposition were not immune from the importance or necessity to quell public fears. For that reason, it became a priority to engender trust back into government and its ministers. However, the strategy employed might easily have been misinterpreted as something that attacked the public or at the very least appeared divisive. Extreme austerity measures sapped any financial power that might have been employed to resist increasingly devastating policies. The introduction of food banks to meet growing numbers of families unable to feed themselves another distraction from the realities of corruption within government.

While the public was told that hard decisions needed to be made it was them who suffered. Heat or eat quickly became the phrase of the time. The PM of the day suggesting people wear an extra jumper to fend off the cold while speaking from his centrally heated home paid for with public money. Daley could still feel the anger he had at the time of listening.

The harder the British public suffered the easier it was for them to forget those in public life living in a different reality. Employing divisive tactics, the Prime Minister initially began by attacking anyone receiving benefits. The elderly and disabled first to experience how easy it was for government propaganda to make them considered as parasites. The gullible masses willing to accept that someone needed to be blamed. Willing to accept that the government knew those responsible and would expose them. Those who knew better and could have argued more strongly against the propaganda did little or nothing to prevent the spread of such lies. Pensioners and the disabled were attacked on streets. It was a bad time that should never have happened, that's what Boris Daley figured.

Over the past dozen years of Tory rule, he had followed each leader with keen interest. Perhaps hoping to witness a change of heart. Hoping that for once the public would be put ahead of Capitalism. So far, and three leaders later Capitalism was winning. However, lately Streaker had appeared to drift. Quite why a mystery. Yet he had been willing to compromise more than any other. A common enough ruse employed by

Political Parties. The closer they got to the next general election the more the public would be tempted to keep them in power via the ballot box.

Daley had seen enough to sense when a government was putting in motion plans to win back support. The first signs a lessening of hardships by acknowledging a need to increase benefits to help the homeless and deprived. However, this time the COVID pandemic had created a need for the National Health Service to be properly provisioned. Years starving it of resources suddenly forgotten. Info had often mused that an entrepreneur might have seized the bull by the horns and turned the UK into a medical miracle for all. A medical aircraft carrier. Free to the indigenous folk and at a cost to foreign patients. Instead of selling armaments the UK could have been the centre of the medical world for state-of-the-art medicine and practices. Quite why no one had felt that way beyond him. Maybe it was being too good towards their fellow man. Something perhaps not included among the values of those able to do it. Certainly, it had nothing to do with money. There was more than enough to be made, pharmaceutical companies proof of that! He called it Destruction over Medicine. Perhaps because it had always been that way no one had the desire for change. Pity.

However, something had changed. He was meeting Jonathon Bandip. His car parked in an isolated spot hidden away in Epping Forest as he waited for Bandip's arrival. The Tory Party was upset over Streaker relocating Parliament. Something they considered less prestigious and far more inconvenient it was an unwelcome change. Yet Info understood what Streaker intended. Centralizing Parliament was meant to make it appear more relevant to the northern counties and countries as well as more accessible. If it worked that way, it could benefit everyone. However, leaving the financial sector behind an unwelcome consequence. Westminster had become even more difficult to navigate as a result with few of his usual sources willing to share much of what was happening behind the scenes.

Receiving a call from Bandip had been a breath of fresh air. The PM's fixer not contacting him without something worthwhile to share. The headlights of a car drawing up behind made him squint at the rear-view mirror before the blazing glare turned black. Moments later Bandip joined him. A breath of cold air following him inside before he slammed shut the door. They shook hands COVID forgotten as were masks. Both had been vaccinated unlike a third of the country that continued to wait patiently for vaccinations. The government complained of shortages as Asian and Africans in the community died more often than whites. The poorest regions suffering most of all.

Info automatically doubted anything the government stated until after fact checking their statements more thoroughly than a background check on guards at the Royal Household. For more than a decade they had repeatedly demonstrated a complete lack of compassion for the poor and most vulnerable. Often comparing them to parasites. Changes that were happening today incongruous with their history. He needed to know if they were genuine. Whether the general public were to be given a reprieve from their divisive attitude.

"Nice to see you Jonathon. It's been a while."

Bandip made himself comfortable, "Things are precarious as you no doubt have already surmised for yourself Boris." He said getting straight to the point. "The PM is being hammered by his own Party for doing what the country needs and is looking for support outside Westminster."

"You mean the relocation," he clarified.

"Yes. That's part of it." Having anticipated resistance even Bandip was surprised by how strong the opposition was within the Party including some highly esteemed people. "I know you're a supporter of the relocation and might be willing to demonstrate that support online and through the national press."

"Maybe," he replied. He had known Bandip for many years and liked him. Somehow, he was different to others in the Party. Almost a neutralist unable to support the opposition, perhaps because of family, but never fully behind leaders over the past decade. "I need an honest answer about Streaker."

It was quite something these days in politics for a reporter to expect an honest answer from someone so close to the wheels of power. Bandip felt uplifted that Info considered it possible with him. "I'll try."

"Why is Streaker relocating to Blackburn?" A straightforward question on the surface with a hidden and highly dangerous undercurrent.

The answer not immediate as Bandip played with words in his head. "Streaker sees it, as necessary. The north is about as fed up as it can get with Westminster and the prospect of declarations for independence are rife. Moving Parliament will create a fresh political appearance that will encompass the entire Kingdom."

"That's how it appears on the surface," he said. "But what about personal motives. Why has he been so dogged about doing this and willing to fight off revolt after revolt in his own Party when most would have withdrawn from such confrontations?"

"I believe that he acknowledges it is in the best interests of the country for the relocation to happen. If he does have some personal agenda, he has kept it to himself. Does that answer your question?"

He could do nothing but hope that his faith in Bandip was justified. It just seemed odd that a narcissist would put the country before himself. Yet that appeared to be what he was doing. "Fine," he said. "What do you want from me?"

Bandip handed him a Portable Storage Device (PSD). "You'll find everything you need to support the relocation on this. We'd be grateful if you would begin distributing the data immediately."

Info pocketed the device, "Why come to me and not someone higher up the food chain?"

"Because for this to be accepted by the public we need people like you with a proven history of independence from the Establishment."

"You had me even before this conversation began. It is a good idea and benefits us all."

He might have saved him from revealing his personal opinion but Bandip guessed Info survived by wringing honesty from people like him. Hearing his opinion counted. "In that case I think we're done."

"Not quite," Info said. "There's a rumour that one of your ministers is arranging a contract with Bus Internals Limited to supply a hundred buses specifically to run between London, Blackburn and Edinburgh. The amount quoted me was sixty thousand pounds per bus. So, six million quid."

"I'm not involved in that particular issue but imagine there must be plenty of transportation issues being worked out."

"That's what I thought too, but are you aware that Bus Internals Limited doesn't manufacture or sell buses? They manufacture seats and handrails for buses, that's all. Also, the person holding fifty one percent shares in the company is Lord Horny."

"Where's this going," Bandip sensed nothing good.

"The bus manufacturer BIL are dealing with is Chinese based."

"You're suggesting something untoward is happening?"

"I'm telling you what I know but like me you've already picked up on the possibilities. However, I'll keep digging now that I'm aware of Lord Horny's involvement. Someone from the House of Lords shouldn't have fifty one percent interest in a company that the government is about to spend six million quid with. Neither should the government be dealing with a 'middle-man' for Chinese goods when they could be dealing directly with bus manufacturers in the UK."

"What do you want me to do?"

"Speak to the Transport minister, Basil Dence. Tell him that he's headed towards a cliff edge if the deal goes through."

"That sounds remarkably like blackmail Boris," Bandip smiled without humour.

"Not at all. I'm warning you that I'll keep digging and bring what I find out in the open. Of course, unless you choose to ignore it because it's all fine. I consider it as helping Streaker rather than hindering him."

Sometimes it's best to pull back even when your blood makes you feel angry. He nodded and silently climbed out of the car returning to his own.

CHAPTER FIVE

Naughty boys

The room felt sombre. A grey sky lighting it in a way that reflected poorly off its wood panelled walls making it necessary for the interior lights to be on. Sat behind his large oak desk Streaker appeared to be brooding. Standing behind him Jonathon Bandip appeared neutral. Waiting to do his PMs bidding.

"Basil you were present eighteen months ago when I instructed that no contracts relating to the relocation should be passed without first receiving scrutiny from Bernard Allfores."

"Yes, Prime Minister," Basil Dence timidly replied. Hating the fact that he was about to be reprimanded by someone he admired most. It shouldn't have happened. He shouldn't be here. He had been forced into doing what he did by family.

"Yet you still took it on yourself to ignore my instructions. Almost signing off a contract with a bus company that doesn't have any buses just seats and handrails." How Streaker retained his composure was a tribute to his many years in politics. He was furious. His anger warranted. Bernard Allfores had agreed to keep silent about the affair between his wife and Streaker provided all conditions of their agreement were kept. One being that he would select all major companies to be involved in the relocation. Had Dence signed the contract with Bus Internals Limited Allfores would have been free to expose the lies Streaker had used on the public. It would have been catastrophic. His ambition for a statue of himself outside the relocated Parliament standing no chance of success.

"Lord Horny made it sound less like an issue directly involved with the relocation. The buses were merely passing through Blackburn on their way to Scotland." Dence spoke humbly. A man swimming in an ocean without any sign of land.

"Of all my ministers Basil you were the least I would have expected to behave in such a way. Disregarding my instructions so blatantly is an act of mutiny!"

"But…."

"I haven't finished," he snapped. "What did Horny offer you?"

Dence hesitated. "Me nothing. My brother the contract to transport the buses and maintenance supplies over the next three years from China to the UK."

The left eyebrow on Streaker's face rose a quarter inch. Nothing for himself. He was doing it for family. Something Streaker was familiar with. He leaned back. Expression less intimidating. "The pressures of family life can be a burden at times. We've all been there. You should have come to me."

"Yes, Prime Minister," Dence stared down at the desk unable to meet his gaze.

"The good thing is that the contract wasn't signed."

He looked up. Hope in his eyes. "No, it wasn't. I was meant to sign it by tomorrow."

"Not going to happen Basil. Jonathon is going to send it up to Allfores and we'll wait to hear back from him whether it's agreed. Although I have no doubt, he'll throw it out." Streaker took a deep breath. "Look on this incident as a close call Basil and make certain it's never repeated. Do not speak to Lord Horny about it I'll deal with him myself."

"Yes, Prime Minister." He rose from the seat at left their meeting concluded.

"Do you want me to ask Lord Horny to visit you here?"

Streaker shook his head, "No. You don't call someone like him to your office for a bollocking. Find out where he is this afternoon and have my car ready. He owes me and I intend to collect."

A call on his direct line interrupted them. Bandip tactfully left him alone.

A cultured voice oozing with sophistication by way of an overindulgent upbringing made a familiar introduction, "Rupert it's Jerome. You appear to be taking your job too seriously."

Jerome Shylocke the most senior banker in the United Kingdom preferred a reclusive existence. One in which he delegated every issue that required his attention for resolution by underlings. They had spoken previously on a couple of occasions but never over his direct line. That the conversation had begun with Shylocke's rumoured format expressing displeasure an indication that Streaker needed to heed a warning.

"I won't take up too much of your valuable time Rupert," a hint of superiority in his tone that irritated Streaker. "You're not allowing traditional construction industry employers to be used in the Re-location Project. That's a mistake that I hope you'll rectify immediately."

"No," Streaker replied attempting to disguise the genuine fear racing through his body.

"That's disappointing," Shylocke replied. "I thought you more astute. You've submitted several other projects requiring financial support....."

"I have a plan to..."

"I don't like being interrupted Prime Minister!" The articulated tone rose unusually higher stressing he stop before saying more. "As I stated your government has submitted several other projects seeking financial investment. Are you really willing to put them in jeopardy over this temporary fixation you have of doing things honestly?"

Streaker remained silent.

"You can answer now," Shylocke told him.

It was as if he were back in school. The Headmaster listening to an explanation why he had been a bad boy. He didn't like it. He was the British Prime Minister for heaven's sake! "What are you suggesting Jerome?"

"I thought I'd made myself plain enough but to clarify start using traditional contractors for the Relocation Project. Do you understand?"

"I'll give your suggestion the consideration it deserves," he replied.

"Make certain that you do Prime Minister, you won't like the alternative."

Their conversation ended abruptly with Shylocke cradling his handset. Streaker did the same more slowly. The top banker had power, enormous power, more than even the Prime Minister. To defy him would take nerve but he needed more than that to win. He needed a strategy. A plan that would allow him to continue with what he had begun without interference. Shylocke had fired a warning shot across his bow the next would cripple him in some way before a final ruthless strike would forever remove him. Everything he had worked towards would be lost. Gone as if it never existed.

CHAPTER SIX

The Devil's in the detail

Drowning in opulence was the way members of the Panda Private Male Club situated in Park Lane wanted to feel. An ultra-exclusive club that met the needs of anyone with the funds to pay an annual fee of a quarter million pounds. Catering to the needs of its membership meant that none were ever alone while in the building. An attractive personal assistant assigned to them immediately they stepped through the oak wood entrance. Ready to cater to their every need while on the premises. Fixtures and furnishing styled from a previous century intended to accentuate when male domination could easily ignore female equality. No expense had been spared in its creation or modernization since 1895.

A waft of leather touched his nostrils as Streaker strolled into a small reading room his bodyguard close behind. Its only occupant the man he had come to see. No personal assistant. Meaning he was expected.

Lord Selwyn Horny sat alone among two dozen empty green leather armchairs his head buried behind a copy of The Times newspaper. His balding scalp just visible. Streaker instructed his bodyguard to remain by the door before he crossed the room to join him. What needed to be said not for the ears of minions. Occupying an armchair opposite, he coughed politely for the other man to acknowledge his presence.

The newspaper gently rustled but did not come down, "I've been expecting you Prime Minister. Although I'm surprised you maintain your membership." The thin paper division all that separated their self-importance. Although not sufficient to keep a mutual disdain contained. Their loathing for one another full of energy they sensed capable of touch.

He had never found anything to like about Horny and it appeared the same could be said for the Lord about Streaker. Their mutual dislike had been immediate. As if they had hated one another from some other place. "Are we really going to talk through your paper?"

The paper came down with a more obvious rustle. Horny's dark green eyes defiant. Challenging. Arrogance that knew no bounds. A ruddy complexion with pock marked skin made him appear aggressive. Dangerous even. While sixty years of overindulgence had turned him pudgy. Thick fingers with gold rings and a wrist wearing a Rolex statements of wealth. Below a balding top thin strands of greying hair remained at the sides brushed over his ears, while he allowed hair at the back to grow long. Silver grey curls snaking over his shirt collar. Oddly untidy above a black pinstripe Armani suit. A modern look. Untidy wealth. He knew exactly why Streaker was there but asked the question anyway. "I come here for an hour every day. It's where I like to recharge my batteries after spending time at the Lords. Why are you here Rupert?"

It occurred to him to ask how long he had spent at the House of Lords after receiving his £325 daily attendance fee. Horny visited the Lords daily, that much he was aware, collecting the daily fee no matter how long spent there. Sometimes just a brief five minutes to sign the register before leaving to do business elsewhere. A reason Horny was so opposed to the relocation and the disbandment of the Lords in favour of the newly proposed Second Chamber. Losing more than £1500 per week would have been a significant loss to any mere mortal but meant little to a billionaire such a Horny. For him it was the prestige and power that meant everything. Controlling the lives of millions to his own personal agenda. A selfish craving. "You attempted to use my Transport Minister to push through a contract with a firm you have a fifty one percent investment. Dence should have told you that every contract related to the relocation has to pass through Bernard Allfores. I made that plain to all my Ministers."

"He did tell me," Horny admitted disdainfully. No fear or apology in his eyes.

"Yet you still attempted to go against my instructions in order to profit from a contract that would have cost the public millions of pounds."

"Nothing that you haven't done yourself in the past," he reminded him. It pleased him to do so and he smiled hoping to irritate Streaker. No one was totally without sin. Something Streaker was all too aware as he chose his reply carefully.

"You seem to think you have control Selwyn," Streaker noted. "It's a mistake many make with me. But you're forgetting something that happened only eighteen months ago between your son and a Jennifer Juggs."

"I haven't forgotten. It's just no longer important to me. I disowned Horace about three months ago. He's on his own. Went off with a woman I forbade him to touch. He means nothing do your worst. I don't care. I'm done with you stamping around Westminster as though you own it. You don't! Your time will soon be finished, and you'll just be another painting on a wall. History."

Disowning his own son because he didn't as he was told sounded like an eighteenth-century tradition. But to Selwyn Horny and his family it remained a way of life. However, deriding a sitting Prime Minister was something else. Something that could not be tolerated.

"You're a dinosaur Selwyn. It's time you joined us in the twenty first century. How you treat your son reflects how you view the world around you. Nothing exposes a a has-been more than the way they treat family."

Horny moved uncomfortably pushing the newspaper away on the table between them. "I don't need family guidance from a man who has the moral code of a rabbit. As for the contract with BIL, it's a good one worth every penny even your friendly cuckold husband Allfores will appreciate that!"

Streaker remained calm but it was a struggle. Horny knew which buttons to press to start a fire. But this was one argument he was determined to win and losing his temper an unaffordable luxury. His response was cold. Brittle. Steel edged. "Before I leave number ten you and your cronies will be redundant. You're powerless to stop it. The public are behind me. The Second

Chamber is coming. The House of Lords consigned to the past."

"What are you really up to?" Horny snapped. "I think you're a Republican like you're American chum. Seeing yourself as President of the UK."

Streaker wouldn't admit it, but the thought had indeed crossed his mind. Doing away with the monarchy after the House of Lords seemed a possible next step making way for a completely new political era of Republicanism and who better placed to be the first President than him? "That's ridiculous. Say it loud enough for all to hear and people will realise just how much of a bad loser you really are Selwyn. You're going to miss the power the Lords gave you and I'm going to enjoy watching it slip from your hands."

"There's still time for things to change Rupert. Each day at Westminster is an opportunity for me to dethrone you and I won't stop until I do!"

Streaker smiled sympathetically, "I'm sure you're going to be too busy worrying about HMRC," he replied with unconcealed satisfaction. "My Office has dropped an investigation on their desk regarding some of your foreign business dealings." He rose from the seat as Horny's jaw dropped open. No words needed. His eyes said everything Streaker needed to know. "I expect they'll soon be in touch. Good luck Selwyn. You're going to need it."

No one liked the idea of having the tax man digging around in their personal cess pool especially a fat cats. As normal Bandip had been thorough and identified several indiscretions related to business dealings with both the Chinese and Russians not easily answered.

Deep satisfaction followed Streaker to his car as he called Bandip. "All done."

"Glad to hear it Rupert. Did you mention Jerome Shylocke?"

"No. We need to deal with him with more subtlety. I want you to discuss his threat against me with Boris Daley. Tell him to write a short article from an anonymous source that points to a certain top-level Banker as threatening the Prime Minister to help traditional contractors obtain work in the Relocation Project or lose the financial support of banks in other projects."

"Isn't that extreme?" Bandip said concerned. Taking on a bank was not something anyone did without credible evidence, including the British Prime Minister.

"The phone conversation was recorded," Streaker said allaying his fears.

"Surprising Shylocke would let himself be recorded."

"At any other time, he wouldn't, but the man's an arrogant, pompous arse who thinks he can threaten anyone he fancies including me!" His temper matched his tone. "He needs to be slapped down and I intend to be the PM who sees it happens. Also, arrange a meeting for me as soon as possible with Brian Belter at the Bank of England. If anyone can crush Shylocke it will be him." The new Head of the Bank of England had earned a reputation as a tough negotiator who gave little wriggle room to those who broke or bent the rules whilst serving at the Financial Conduct Authority over a ten-year period.

"You're getting out the big guns," Bandip joked.

"Do something else for me. Find out who Horace Horny has gone off with. Apparently, he's been disowned by his father because of her. It might prove useful to know in the future."

CHAPTER SEVEN

A meeting of minds

Bernard Allfores and Boris Daley were strangers. Jonathon Bandip arranged for them to meet for a minimum hour. The idea behind their meeting to prove Streaker's intentions were genuine. That the Prime Minister really did want what was best for the country not just himself. In the event that he secured public enthusiasm for his premiership by winning the 2024 general election merely an endorsement that he had proven himself as the right man for the time. Mimicking his wartime hero Winston Churchill.

The two men sat facing one another in the portacabin that was Allfores temporary office at the relocation site outside Blackburn. Using wooden chairs to sit and a desk to lean on and rest their steaming coffee mugs. The temperature cool but not uncomfortable.

"I have to admit that I've never been interviewed by the Press," Allfores began.

"Promise it won't hurt," Daley grinned. "First off why you?"

"What does that mean?"

"I mean why do you think out of all the people the PM could have chosen he selected you for the job?"

"He told me he thinks I'm right for the job. After eighteen months I'm hoping that I'm proving him right."

"Do you think he had sex with your wife?"

Allfores had been expecting the question. It reflected what every media outlet kept asking. He had thought about it so much lying came out like a muscle memory reaction, without delay. "No."

"Yet you and your wife are separated?"

"Yes."

"Okay, that's the gutter press investigation over with," Daley said. Not expecting anything better than Allfores had given him. "You were recently sent a contract from the Transport Minister regarding a fast bus service using BIL. Have you had time to review it?"

"Yes," he replied. So far, he had no reason to feel comfortable speaking to the reporter. Mention of his personal circumstance still raw and painful. Quite why Bandip had thought they might get along a mystery.

"Is it likely to receive your support?" Daley asked reading the other man's body language. Arms currently folded across his chest. A natural defence posture. Allfores was uncomfortable but it was understandable given the personal nature of the questions so far. He knew that he would need to lead their conversation. Bring it to a level less likely to cause concern. Years of experience instinctively told him that he was dealing with someone untainted by a political skill set.

Allfores turned and pointed towards an eighteen-inch pile of paperwork, "Those are hard copies of all proposals I've received from ministers at Westminster since I started. I wanted to keep a hard copy record to show people what happens when you get put in charge of a project like this."

"Have they all been accepted?" Daley asked, surprised by the small mountain of paper. Eighteen months of recommendations with a few backhanders thrown in no doubt.

"None. The proposal you mention relating to BIL among them. As much as Basil Dence praises the use of this company which by the way is fifty one percent owned by Lord Horny. It's already too dated against what I have in mind. The offer is for terrestrial transport which will in the not-too-distant future prove too problematic."

Daley frowned intrigued, "Aren't all bus services terrestrial?"

"As a reporter you must regularly look at what's happening to our planet. What do you think will be a consistent future weather issue in the north of this country?"

"Flooding?" He guessed, the suggestion falling from his lips without a second thought.

"Exactly," Allfores smiled. Finally, they agreed on something that diverted him away from Kate Allfores and Streaker. "It's why we're in discussion with a Canadian company called Skytrain. It offers a driverless fully automated train system running on elevated guideways, that allow unprecedented high reliability both in terms of train scheduling and endurance."

"But it's a train not a bus?"

"It's the future." Allfores sighed gravely. An expression that he had spent a great deal of time considering the pros and cons before selecting an answer. Not given to radical thought for the sake of it he had played with dozens of scenarios in which terrestrial bus services might prove a viable option. Each time they failed to meet his criteria. "Wherever Parliament is relocated must be accessible twenty-four hours of every day from London to Edinburgh. That was my criteria. My goal." He paused momentarily recovering memories of nights spent looking through countless articles about all-weather transport until concluding the one most appropriate for the UK. "There is a very real and serious threat of flooding due to climate change. The north of England is where we might be hit worst of all. Terrestrial transportation will always be vulnerable, while our proposed elevated design with its cocooned protection offers an all-weather system."

"How high from the ground are you intending to build it?"

"Fifty feet."

"Wow, what about winds?"

"The cocoon protection is a revolutionary aerodynamic design tested against two hundred mile an hour winds. Ninety five percent of wind is prevented from doing damage. Additionally, the supporting steel pillars are planted deep underground and also aerodynamically moulded to avoid wind damage. With our high expectations of flooding all supporting architecture is also marine ready." He paused to allow Daley time to absorb the details before continuing. "We need this form of Skytrain to ensure that the relocation of Parliament is never cut off during winter months. Buses and trains are all vulnerable and though it comes at increased cost it will pay for itself due to its all-weather capability."

"How do you expect to pay for it? I mean it's not going to be cheap?"

"We're going to take a leaf out of the Canadian's book to meet costs. Advertising will be huge. Passenger charges low set against a maximum five-minute wait between trains. Each train will consist of four carriages. The run between London and Blackburn will consist of fifty-three stations and another fifty-three between Blackburn and Edinburgh. Due to the frequency of the service, we estimate an ability to move one hundred thousand passengers per day."

"Why fifty-three stations?"

"It's part of our Canadian initiative to mimic how it's being done already so that we can better assess passenger flows, maintenance costs and so on. By following what the Canadians have achieved we're in a good position to argue a strong case for Skytrain. Additionally, Thailand also use the service with even larger passenger counts. However, because we want to mirror the Canadians as much as possible. Fifty-three is the number of stations serviced around Vancouver. Keeping to the same number of stations allows us some latitude in gauging schedules while also providing access to people in rural areas who will never have had such an experience. Offering rural communities, a public transport system in many instances for the first time will get people out of their cars and thereby help clean up the environment. It was one of Streaker's priorities."

"Sounds to me as if Skytrain is another separate project all on its own that's evolved from the relocation. Streaker actually wanted it?"

"Yes. I can't do anything without his consent. Don't forget he's the one who will seek funding. I need him on side before I could even consider taking this on. Fortunately, he was head of me in regards improving the environment. Whatever you might think of him he is forward thinking."

"Are conversations with Streaker ever difficult for you given the initial allegations that he had sex with your wife?"

"All contact between us is through Jonathon. I haven't spoken to Streaker since I accepted this job. He's a busy man as am I."

"But isn't that a little odd given the size and importance of this project?"

"Maybe, but it works. I keep him up-to-speed with what I'm doing and if he doesn't agree I'm sure I'd be the first to hear about it. He seems satisfied that my judgement fits in with his overview regarding the relocation."

"What about your wife. She's managing the old Parliament buildings and play a significant rolo in the disbandment of the House of Lords as well as the relocation of MPs and their staff to the new site. Are you in regular contact with her?"

"Of course," he said. Tone neutral.

"How are you finding working together?" Daley had just got Allfores to lower his arms from his chest, yet they appeared on the rise again.

"Any difficulties we might have shared are behind us now. I'd say our work relationship is better than most. We understand our roles and our approaches to the issue in front of us. In that way we make a good team."

"Thanks for your frankness Bernard. Now please tell me more about the next stages of the construction." He said as Allfores arms dropped again.

CHAPTER EIGHT

Prime Minister for a reason

A week after the meeting between Allfores and Daley Streaker found himself studying plans for Skytrain wondering whether there was an opportunity to make even more use of it.

Allfores had proven incredibly useful highlighting the possibilities of more frequent stations in rural areas. In economic terms it might be argued as a new income stream reached by providing untapped thousands with a cheap frequent public transport service that allowed them access to the large cities and areas they might otherwise have reached by road or indeed never visited. In addition, schools and other academic entities would likewise be more accessible and therefore likely to attract students willing to look further than their front doorstep. Another win for the economy. Why he hadn't seen it before a mystery. Skytrain could be used as a means of connecting the country like no other and, importantly, gave the car a secondary place when travelling.

The infrastructure costs for electrifying the motoring world still a headache that defied all planned schedules his government had suggested. One lie too many he thought. The current notion of no fossil fuelled vehicles being manufactured in the UK by 2030 might be possible but how on earth to power them an obstinate impossibility. Approximately 35 million Electric Vehicles (EV) required twenty operational nuclear power stations to avoid power cuts to homes and industry. The UK currently had six with two more entering the energy theatre in the next twelve months and another possibly beginning construction early the following year. Nuclear power stations generally took 9.4 years to build which meant he was well past a time when it might have been possible. Leaders didn't receive a statue for failure.

However, Skytrain could be run within their power architecture and by ignoring the needs of EV infrastructure could continue to connect other parts of the including Northern Ireland. His dream for a bridge from Scotland to Northern Ireland had never waned. Skytrain would be a start making the countries accessible for their peoples a necessary first step. Living in Belfast while working in Edinburgh or vice versa was a game changer the North could not ignore. For the moment it was necessary to forget about products and other material things. People is what drove an economy and allowing them freedom of movement an essential part of it. That's something the European Union (EU) had recognized but failed to properly orchestrate. Once again too many greedy hands on the reins of power. The rush for change a massive mistake that ignored the mindset formed by centuries of nationalism. Recognizing and accepting the existence of a nationalist influence and allowing it to continue a necessary part of bringing peoples closer. The UK could make their dream a reality within the confines of its smaller borders. Let the people call themselves Scots, Welsh, Northern Irish, or English. It didn't matter. The fact was they were a part of something bigger – the UK. It's what would be most important over time as generations passed. Once people grew accustomed to the accessibility Skytrain provided it would quickly become the *norm*. Travel between Scotland and Belfast for employment routine no matter the job or status.

Against all claims that the UK could not stand alone in the modern world. He could envisage a UK that could most definitely do so through a process of self-reconstruction. Making Northern Ireland more accessible key to his plans because of its connection with the United States and expanse of agricultural land that could make the UK self-sufficient for food. Additionally, the prospect of trading with the EU through the Republic another bonus

However, even with all the potential benefits made obvious in discussion with his own people resistance from them continued to mount threatening to deny him any possibility of a statue erected in his honour outside the new parliament buildings. Reaching for the phone he called Helen Healthy the only MP representing the Green Party.

"Always nice to get a call from you Prime Minister," she said with laughter in her voice, leaving him guessing whether the sentiment were true.

"I wanted your opinion on something."

"I'm honoured," her tone unmistakably genuine.

"Bernard Allfores has been doing a remarkable job with the Relocation of Parliament Project. The costs are down. The timescale is on course as predicted. Businesses are thriving and people in the area feel good about what's happening. Well, most of them anyway, I know there have been arguments over the Green Belt land that's been occupied, but apart from that the man at the top of the project has conducted himself better than expectations."

"I agree, he's doing a very good job. I'm sure the public appreciate his efforts."

"I want him to be nominated for an award, but it might not look bi-partisan if I'm the one who puts his name forward."

"You want me to do it?"

"I think it would reflect how Westminster as a whole appreciate his efforts if you were the one responsible for asking he be considered."

"What type of award were you thinking?"

"An OBE."

"Fine. Thank you for thinking of me. It will be a pleasure."

He cradled the handset a smile of self-satisfaction twisting his lips. Honouring Allfores would stifle some of the opposition against the project, especially as the Green's would be his sponsors. No one could deny Allfores success and with it the notion to keep arguing against the relocation would, he hoped, lose some impetus.

CHAPTER NINE

Cabinet Meeting – For the good of the country

Cabinet meetings were commonly a place for government ministers to unanimously choose the best direction government steer the country. However, over the past year something had changed. The Prime Minister less willing to use traditional contractors at the heart of the change for mutual agreement. The off-white room prepared for the 10:00 meeting was naturally light and airy because of large floor-to-ceiling windows with three brass chandeliers alight hanging from the ceiling high above.

Twenty-two ministers sat gathered round a magnificent boat-shaped table purchased during the Gladstone era. Centred in green baize of exquisite texture above sturdy oak legs. The chairs around it solid mahogany, also dating back to Gladstone. It was the epitome of British manufacturing. Only the prime minister's seat, placed in front of the marble fireplace, possessed arms that made it easy to recognise. The decor of the cabinet room was a lesson in less appearing to be more. A solitary portrait of Sir Robert Walpole by

Jean Baptiste van Loo hung over the fireplace – the only display of a globally significant history. The ministers' appointment as members of Her Majesty's Most Honourable Privy Council allowed them the use of term 'The Right Honourable', while their seating arrangement at the table reflected seniority.

Basil Dence was determined to win back the confidence of his Prime Minister. Although unknowingly he had never possessed it. His long-term admiration for Rupert Streaker as blinkered as his view of his own limited capabilities or the influence his family possessed to ensure him a seat at the Cabinet table. "My proposal as forwarded to your Office Prime Minister and circulated to other members of the Cabinet offers a means by which government could begin a new income stream that remains untouched."

Streaker looked at his computer screen and proposal relating to the cyclist tax sent him. There was no doubt it had been thoroughly examined or that the figures showed a more than reasonable potential revenue. Dence had used Northern Ireland as an example. With an estimated 600,000 cyclists and a proposal for the introduction of a £10 pedal cyclist tax it offered a fresh revenue of £6,000,000 per annum from the country.

"It won't prove popular among the cyclist community," Kevin Knowall, Minister for Education said. Himself a keen cyclist.

"Cyclists are the only road users that receive a free pass to travel wherever they want. Cycle lanes, parking rails and the maintenance of both." Dence argued.

"Those are paid for by local authorities from local taxes," Knowall replied.

"And that's why it's unfair," Dence continued, surprisingly confident. "Cycle users specifically need to pay for what they use as does everyone else. It's not fair to lumber local communities with a tax for a service that a majority in those communities will never use."

"You can't argue that a majority will never use a cycle to get from A to B."

"Very few of those you indicate will be seventy years of age or older. So, that's the first group who shouldn't be taxed for cycle lanes and so on. Then we have people who simply don't use cycles. Using Northern Ireland as an example indicates that only twelve percent of the total population are cyclists. Whatever way you look at it a large number of the population contribute towards cyclists who themselves are in the minority. Additionally, cyclists are one of the most vulnerable of road users. Each year more than one hundred cyclists die on our roads while a further three thousand are injured. The cost on the NHS is huge. Yet most cyclists continue to use roads free of charge."

"What about the environmentalists, they're going to oppose this. Cycles are clean transport for the climate. Taxing them will put many off using them and arguably return to their cars instead." Knowall, who arrogantly looked down on every other colleague as not his equal in intelligence. Felt uncomfortably irritated arguing with who many considered as least intelligent among them.

"The country needs to collect more money to pay for COVID. Cyclists offer a genuine way by which that's possible. Arguments are stronger than for many other suggestions this Cabinet has entertained," Dence finished.

"How do you propose it be administered?" Felicity Hangready, the Home Secretary asked.

"They're road users it would be administered by the Department of Vehicles and Licensing Centre (DVLC). What we're discussing is nothing more than a form of road licence. No reason for it to come from anywhere else."

"You're cyclist road tax is too low," Malcolm Market the Trade Minister said. "It needs to increase to twenty-five pounds a licence. That would equate to fifteen million from your Northern Irish example rather than six. That kind of income could genuinely be useful to help with the costs we're faced from COVID."

"What about opposition," Knowall argued. "It's bound to be fierce."

"Only cyclists support cyclists the rest of us are fed up with the buggers!" Roger Rabid Chief Tory Whip added. "If we argue that cyclists are not paying their way how many non-cyclists do you suppose will support us?"

"Policing will need to be provided additional powers to stop and check cyclists for licences," Hangready said. "Also, I believe it's about time that cyclist insurance is made mandatory. The statistics relating to deaths and injuries urges us to do so."

"I agree," Streaker said with a murmur of agreement from most others at the table. "We can leave it to the insurance companies to form their own policies to meet any mandate that we decide together with appropriate costs."

"You're forcing many people off their cycles by introducing such things," Knowall said.

"No more than we had to do with personal vehicles. COVID has created extraordinary times for all of us. All of us need to adapt for us to make progress and get back to normality, but it's not going to happen overnight. I expect it to take another five years before we'll be able to put the pandemic properly behind us."

"You think the public are going to accept that?"

"I think the public like us have no choice," he replied. "Let's see a vote of hands Streaker said. "Who are for pursing a cycle tax further?" Eighteen hands rose. "To those of you in opposition your stance is noted. However, we will be taking it forward."

Dence sat back elated he had won. Knowall unhappy in defeat.

Streaker read from the agenda in front of him. "Next. COVID where are we in regards a third of the people who have not yet received vaccinations?"

Terence Remedy, Health Minister looked up from the table. COVID had dogged his experience as Health Minister. No one else wanted the job even now with the vaccination being distributed. Delays by drug manufacturers caught between foreign and indigenous demands for vaccines overwhelming them. "We should be receiving more vaccine tomorrow in the areas it's most needed."

"How many people will receive the vaccination over the coming week?" Streaker asked.

It was the kind of question Remedy expected but loathed. Almost each time he had provided estimates they had proven incorrect. It was beyond embarrassing. His career would always be stained. History likely to view him as an incompetent. That no other Health Minister had ever stumbled through such a difficult period no longer a defence in the eyes of the public. After more than two years living with the COVID meant that both he and the public no longer attracted the luxury of inexperience. He was expected to demonstrate a highly professional management covering all aspects of vaccine supply and distribution. Nothing less. The fact it wasn't happening might not be directly his fault, but it reflected gaps in a system that he agreed. Gaps that should not exist. He coughed before speaking. A sign of nervousness. "I hope to have two hundred thousand a day vaccinated in the areas that have so far not received sufficient vaccine by the end of the week. Provided no further delays occur in the supply chain."

"What are you doing to ensure that no further delays occur?" Streaker asked.

Another question he knew would be asked. Another he loathed. "I've put in place instructions intended to warn us in the even there's a disruption in supply. However, the manufacturers have given their assurances that they now have sufficient vaccine to fulfil our demand."

"I want you to keep the pressure on them to meet their assurances. I do not want to have to face the public again with excuses," he said, a touch of irritation in his tone. With only two years before the next election, he could not afford questions about his government's competent ability to deal with the pandemic a headline presented by the opposition. Streaker moved on to the next agenda item. "The relocation of Parliament appears to be on target. Bernard Allfores demonstrating that he was the right choice."

"Not everyone agrees with your logic to move to Blackburn Prime Minister," Mary Munch Minister for the Environment, Food and Rural matters said in a challenging tone that none could miss.

Streaker did not immediately reply. Munch was a known accomplice of those intent on stopping the relocation. Powerful figures who remained determined to stop the relocation at any cost. Lord Horny undoubtedly one of the leaders and close friend of the Munch family. The forty something Munch stared across the table with a sign of defiance none of her colleagues would dare.

Her green eyes narrowed. Long dyed black hair curled around slender shoulders above a smart fawn trouser suit. "I appreciate the concerns of those who do not want the relocation, but we've already moved on. We need to discuss what it will mean and how we can make the most of what the relocation offers."

"It offers nothing for most of us Prime Minister," Munch said flatly. The room silent. Atmosphere tense.

Ordinarily Streaker would have dismissed Munch without hesitation. However, doing so did not dismiss opposition to the relocation. Besides, he preferred keeping enemies close. "I hope the latest news about Skytrain will change your view."

"People are concerned that our established circle of construction suppliers are being ignored in favour of companies selected by Allfores that have no understanding of how government operates." It was a common argument used by those losing out from a commercial relationship that previously provided credit from a grateful business.

"Then it's about time we showed others how government operates. The larger the commercial circle the more chance we have of improving the tenders we receive. Additionally, by allowing other smaller businesses to get involved government is helping to support business on a broader scale.

Doing so underlines our approach to business as stated in our Party manifesto."

"But doing so hurts the relationship with our established contractors." She argued.

"How so?" Streaker asked innocently

"They have expectations in regards potential contracts. Their future plans involve contracts they should rightly expect from government. Not passing on those contracts makes it difficult for them to easily identify projections should they require bank loans."

"Are you suggesting that our established contractors include government contracts in their projections even before they receive such contracts?" He stared at her with a dare in his dark eyes that warned her to answer carefully.

"Some may do," she answered realizing the danger of confirming they did. No company could or should expect a government contract before it was authorized. The idea a company might do so implied it had reason to believe it would do so without receipt of official authorization. How that was possible either a risk or road that led to corruption.

"They might be willing to take the risk of suggesting such a thing for a bank loan, but I believe to do so is fraudulent or are you suggesting corruption within government is allowing such things to happen?"

Munch felt her cheeks flush. Streaker had guided her to the edge of a cliff. Was she about to jump? "I'm merely suggesting that a company that has done a good job for government should feel they have a good chance of receiving additional work."

Streaker studied her. The room silent. People holding their breath. "Quite right Mary, but they shouldn't take it for granted. Don't you agree?"

"Of course, Prime Minister." She said. Tone timid.

"Good." He grinned. A win. One that would be repeated to others in the Party. "The world is changing Mary. All of us need to accept that and adapt. For example, Skytrain offers a genuinely all-weather transport facility to reach from one end of the country to the other twenty-four hours a day. I believe it to be the future for cross country travel."

"What about bus services?" Market asked.

"Relegated to city travel only. Same as coaches. Skytrain offers an inexpensive transport system that has proven highly reliable in both Canada and Thailand. Cross country travel for commuters will become something many have never experienced. Accessible, fast, and reliably on time. Taking them from London to Blackburn stopping at fifty-three new stations never previously catered for and on to Edinburgh stopping at another new fifty-three stations. We're opening up the country and by doing improving its economy with the introduction of so far untapped indigenous folk."

No one spoke. All attempting to grasp the reality of Streaker's statement. Some recognized the potential almost immediately others took a little longer. After a minute of two Market said, "I like it Prime Minister."

The music and lyrics of *'There'll be blue birds over the white cliffs of Dover'* sung by Vera Lynn suddenly interrupted proceedings. Streaker apologized as he answered the mobile. His wife Jessica on sounded hysterical, "You must come at once. Dolly is lying unmoving on the floor. It spotted Winston in the hall. I don't know CPR. You do. Please Rupert. I need you!"

"I'm in the middle of a Cabinet meeting Jessica. Matters of State are being discussed. The police are CPR trained get one to help they're much closer than I am. Let me know what happens. I'll be up as soon as I can."

The connection went dead. He raised his eyes to meet those of the bewildered people gazing in his direction, some ready to leave.

"CPR?" Remedy asked.

"One of Jessica's parrots dropped off its perch after spotting a cat. It's on the floor. She thinks it needs resuscitation."

A sigh of relief that the patient was not human followed.

"Can a parrot receive CPR?" Munch asked.

"It has a heart," Remedy shrugged.

"Okay, let's return to Skytrain," Streaker said, determined to resume the argument he had been winning before the call. All thought of the parrot already forgotten.

Malcolm Market had never posed a threat. Always a strong supporter of the Prime Minister. Some considered him a sycophant. However, none thought him a fool. If he recognized merit in Skytrain and Streaker's ambitions a third of them automatically fell in line behind him.

"I want Skytrain to become the fundamental base for future transport that we promote. Including for use over a bridge connecting Scotland with Northern Ireland. We desperately need to get people out of their cars. Skytrain is a means by which we can achieve that aim."

"What about EVs won't manufacturers make a fuss that we're not helping with their sales?"

Dence asked carefully. Not wanting to spoil the progress he made with the cycle tax.

"The fact is we can't meet the deadline we've set for the manufacture of all fossil fuelled vehicles to stop by twenty thirty. The infrastructure to meet the demand for thirty-five million vehicles simply won't be there in time. We'll be facing power cuts like we've never experienced unless we do something now. Skytrain is the alternative we need to avoid the power cuts. By the time the relocation is completed Sky train should be up and running between London and Blackburn. The Edinburgh route should enter service eighteen months later. By which time I hope to have secured agreement for a bridge between Scotland and Northern Ireland that will carry both Skytrain and HS Two. Lorries will be loaded onto trains for the journey across. It will revolutionize the North dynamically by making jobs either side of the sea accessible to workers on both sides."

No one had anything to say. Streaker had taken them completely off guard by sharing a vision of the future none had expected.

"And who will be used to construct this network?" Munch asked.

"Allfores is handling all construction work. My understanding is that he intends using local builders under the guidance of Canadian consultants imported to make this build as efficiently accomplished as possible."

"That means you are going to continue to deny access to our established contractors," Munch said, anger bubbling in her tone.

"While I remain Prime Minister that's exactly what will happen. To those of you who don't like it I point towards the number of voters who support the relocation. The latest polls show eighty one percent want this Parliament moved to Blackburn."

No response.

"The next general election is just two years away and I intend to win it. Doing what's agreeable with the public is essential in achieving that aim."

"Even if it damages our traditional commercial relationships?"

"What you need do Mary is impress on our traditional contractors the necessity for us to behave this way. Besides it's only in regards the relocation that we're doing so. Other projects are using their services as usual. They're going to have to be patient."

"What can they expect if we win the election Prime Minister, I mean will what remains of the relocation construction be offered to them?"

"The relocation project will prove to the public that we are doing all we can to reduce costs. Additionally, making Skytrain accessible as public transport in the north will make our next costly projects more acceptable. I'm talking about the bridges connecting Scotland and Northern Ireland. I'm confident that our traditional contractors will want a piece of that action, for that to happen they need to be patient. Do you think you can pass that message on to them?"

Munch momentarily hesitated, "Yes Prime Minister."

After the meeting Streaker made his way upstairs and met his wife where the parrots were kept. Both birds sat on their separate perches with Jessica, his wife, cooing at them.

Hiding his disappointment that both were well took effort. His glossy smile the one he wore when attempting to please the public always a convincing fabrication. "Dolly's back on her perch."

Jessica turned to him, "She passed out. Sight of that cat made her panic. That's what the officer who resuscitated her told me. You should give him a medal for saving her life. His name is PC John Safetyman."

"I'll take that under consideration," he said seriously. He did not miss the irony of handing a medal instead of punishment to someone for saving one of the parrots that he detested. What wo do for love. "How are you?"

"I'm fine now," she said.

"I'm good," Pecker squawked.

He glanced at the bird. A hint of contempt in his eyes.

Jessica moved closer to the bird, "He was so frightened for her."

"I bet," Streaker grimaced.

"They're both so precious," she added.

"Precious," Pecker agreed.

His straight-faced expression might have won an Oscar. It would have been deserved. "At least they're both safe."

She smiled, "I'm sorry to have interrupted you. I appreciate it was the wrong thing for me to do but I panicked when I discovered Dolly on the floor."

He closed an arm around her shoulders pulling her close, "It's fine."

"Shag! Shag!" Pecker squawked.

Streaker closed his eyes bit back an obscenity and turned them towards the door.

CHAPTER TEN

Shadow Cabinet Meeting

Shadow Cabinet meetings occur within the British political system comprising senior members of Her Majesty's Loyal Opposition to analyse their counterparts in Government. Its intention to offer or develop alternative policies, while making Government accountable when its behaviour demands it.

Sitting around an oblong table similar to that of their counterparts except for modern furnishings rather than the historical content. On the table in front of each a laptop. Around them pale walls dressed in portraits of former prominent Labour minister's including Nye Bevan. A Welsh minister recognized as the creator of the National Health Service. While in a corner a mobile tray with white cups and saucers occupying space alongside another with sandwiches covered in cellophane. Expectations the meeting would slip through lunch a forgone conclusion.

Twenty Shadow Ministers had collected to discuss their views relating to a list of Government policies dating back two years that continued to impact the country. Rex Pounding, leader of the opposition coughed to indicate he expected silence before beginning the meeting. Reading from an agenda laid out in front of him he raised the first issue.

"Changes to the tax system by government that do not go far enough to help small businesses continue to miss the mark. More needs to be offered from Banks. The public is still feeling the pain of the two thousand and eight crisis they created because of their greed. The fact that few bankers were ever prosecuted was a part of the deal that banks bend over backwards to do much more for the public especially small businesses in return. Many feel that is not the way things have worked out. Banks all too quickly appear to have forgotten what they owe the public. Has anyone suggestions that we might offer the government as a fresh way to proceed?"

"I have a proposal that's very radical," Alan Akers the Shadow Business Secretary said. "A salary ceiling for all public servants."

"I thought we were fighting to get public servants pay increases?" Fenella Fine Shadow Deputy leader said.

"Increases for those working at the '*coalface*' such as nurses," he agreed. "What I mean are those at the other end of the food ladder, senior staff. It has become increasingly apparent that the division between the most senior and lowest paid staff has grown enormously over the past decade."

"But isn't that simply a reflection of the more difficult demands placed on senior staff?"

Akers could not contain laughter, "I'd say that life and death decisions placed on low paid staff are about as difficult as decisions get."

Fine smiled, "Excuse me for playing Devil's advocate. It's the argument I expect to hear if we go forward with your idea."

"No problem," Akers said. "I do have another agenda behind reducing senior pay sector pay." The room was quiet as he continued. "Society is facing an unprecedented threat from within. One look at what occurred in America over recent years amply demonstrates it. People with too much money able to occupy seats of power to direct a country in the direction they choose."

Pounding asked, "And you're proposing what exactly?"

"Ultimately a counter to billionaires who use their money to attack our system of government. No one in our country should be in such a position."

"You mean you want us to take their money away?"

"I mean I want us to create a threshold relating to how much cash a single individual has at their disposal. Beginning with how much senior public servants should be allowed to be paid. We have to build-in to our political system a mechanism that defends it to such threats. Limiting how much wealth any single individual possesses is a way of achieving that."

"You know what you're suggesting," Pounding said. The implications overwhelming as his mind raced through possibilities. "You want us to attack billionaires and millionaires."

"I want us to bring stability and equality to our country. I want everyone to be less divided by money. I want status to mean something about an individual rather the amount of money in their pocket."

"But is attacking the money they possess credible?"

"I said my approach is radical. It needs to be because the situation we find ourselves in is as I say, unprecedented. There is nothing wrong with us making public servants adhere to a top tier threshold that must never be exceeded. Doing so will allow the lower paid to receive improved pay rises more regularly because the funding needed to do so will have been freed from senior management."

"One argument against doing so is that we will lose the public sector the best people available who will get more in the commercial sector." Fine said.

"That's a rubbish argument and we all know it. We need to stand up against incompetent academics who claim to perform better than the less well educated in the public sector. We need to reward experience and individuals who demonstrate common sense over academic arrogance. Something that has repeatedly failed to meet the demands of working environments. Doing so will act as a lever that prises the public sector away from the influences of wealthy families and Establishment elitism. It's what prevents worthy ordinary individuals from reaching the status they deserve."

"It can't be done," Pounding replied firmly. "It's already been tried and failed. It's called communism. All that occurs is a take-over by a despot bent on power. China and Russia have proven that. Greed for power is the ultimate goal. Humans cannot stop themselves."

"Do you have an alternative?" Akers asked.

"Yes," he replied. "We increase the pay of the lowest paid and keep decreasing the chasm between them and the highest paid. It's no longer good just to pay people to survive from month to month. We need to pay them enough to enjoy some of the luxuries in life. Not everyone is as greedy as those in the highest paid sectors of the community. A majority will be content with enjoying working for a liveable wage that offers access to luxuries without the need for loans. That's where we should be headed rather than the impossible challenge of threatening the wealthy with thresholds."

"Isn't it what we're already doing?" He asked.

"It is," Pounding replied. "And we're being moderately successful as opposed to making no progress at all as would be the case with limiting wealth."

"I think like many others celebrities such as footballers and reality TV stars becoming multi-millionaires is immoral in a country suffering child poverty."

"As do we but must tread carefully if we're to maintain public support. What we're currently doing is the right way, even if progress is slow." Pounding fingered the keyboard in front of him and the screens of his colleagues flashed. "Our aim is to raise the living wage to fifteen pounds an hour by twenty-four. I believe the argument for us to achieve that heady number will motivate public support at the next election. We need to assert that simple survival salaries are no longer acceptable. Companies making millions of pounds in profit need to pay their staff fairly for helping them achieve their goals. The chart in front of you shows the milestone arguments we intend to use from now to twenty-four."

"There will be resistance from employers including government." Akers said reading the figures on the chart.

"This will become one of the biggest political headaches for government. But we must keep to the strategy outlined in front of you to make the most from it. A majority of the public will support us and take note of those who argue against us. Government ministers will be against it because corporations will resist digging into their profits. Small companies will want it because any company employing less than one hundred employees will receive support for their lowest paid workers to ensure their minimum salary meets the fifteen pounds criteria. Funding for it will come from an extra one percent Corporation tax."

"Companies will go ballistic," Akers said.

"Says the man who wanted to limit how much people at the top could earn," Pounding grinned. "For too long large corporations have paid minimalist salaries to help keep their profit margins enormously high to benefit investors. Forcing them to pay a fair wage to their staff who allow them to reach their goals is not rocket science in a world that just suffered a pandemic killing more than a million souls. The poorest in our society have suffered more than any other sector. The poorest in our country include low paid workers. Corporations have been able to avoid fair pay because of consecutive governments allowing them to get away with it including when we were in power. Times are changing, and we have a responsibility to our constituents to ensure they change for the better not worse. Doing so will put us in direct conflict with the most powerful and influential people in this country but I'm not prepared to shy away from them. This Party is going to represent the public in every arena that's necessary to overcome inequality." He paused realizing he was speaking to those already converted. "I apologize for getting on my soap box, but it's my view of our Party and where I want to take it."

"I'm sure we all agree Rex," Susan Scratch the Shadow Chancellor said. "What we want is to win the next election to turn our policies into law. The only way to achieve that aim is by persuading the public that we offer them a way that is both achievable as well as likely to improve the economy. Luckily, Streaker is making the relocation of Parliament a reality which can only help us in regards environment issues and a changing voter dynamic. Moving power out of London will play a significant role in how the North begins to view itself as well as the other countries. For example, Scotland might be less inclined to strike for independence if they see themselves having a bigger say in what the political process."

"You think the relocation will help our Party regain seats in Scotland?" Leonard Lawsuit Shadow Justice Secretary asked.

"If we pursue policies that the public can see for themselves will improve their lives there's no reason to believe otherwise. I certainly think we can have the Scots drop any desire for independence."

"But they want back into the EU and that's not going to happen even if we win the next election. The public voted to be out and I'm beginning to think we should give ourselves a chance. At least ten years to see how the country performs on its own." Lawsuit said.

"Agreed," Pounding added. Some turning to him in surprise. "We need to be making plans for a Federal UK. One that will take us into the next century."

"What about globalization?" Rachel Remote Foreign Secretary asked.

"The EU is not about globalization," Pounding said. "It's about building a Federal State bigger than any other. My predecessor was rightly concerned about its autocratic leadership. Non-elected public servants running the entire thing hidden by bureaucracy and individual state governments. It's not for us. A Federal UK on the other hand would prove a more manageable alternative."

"What about the Royals?"

"They could still have. Perhaps we should use them as done in other European countries. All with a big reduction in cost."

"I'm not sure that would prove popular with the public as many of them are Royal supporters."

"They're the Queen's supporters I'm less convinced they feel the same about any other member of the Royal household, but that will need to be tested."

CHAPTER ELEVEN

The Scots

The Scottish First Minister Bonnie Burns was unhappy over the reconstruction of Hadrian's Wall. The British government was making a statement. Drawing a line with cement and stone that the Scottish public could not ignore. The threat of a relationship about to nosedive unless further attempts at independence were halted. Testing Scottish resolve the ultimate test. Putting the Scottish National Party (SNP) in an unenviable position.

In her official residence Bute House located at 6 Charlotte Square in Edinburgh's New Town itself a part of the First New Town plan unveiled in 1767. Its unified frontage created to blend with other properties in Charlotte Square came as a result of a commission awarded to neoclassical architect Robert Adam in 1791. In 1999 it became the official residence of the First Minister. Sitting at her desk pondering a response to the Hadrian Wall statement Burns was interrupted by her personal aide Patrick Allen.

"There's been an unexpected development at the Wall," he said. Burns looked up from her desk an expectant look in her bright eyes. "The remains of Roman soldiers have been found together with some treasure. It seems one of the dead was a General."

"You suggested a development Patrick. How do you think it will help us?"

"Who keeps the remains and treasure. Currently, Streaker wants it for the museums in England."

"I apologise for my slowness in picking up on where this is headed so please get to the point."

"You should contact the Italians and Pope. Tell them what's been found and suggest they might have an interest in recovering the bodies and treasure."

The implications hit her like a slap on the face. Bringing Rome into the equation created a 'new front' for Streaker to deal with. With so much currently going on he was stretched as it was. Italy and the Pope would undoubtedly be supported by the European Union. The EU grateful for any opportunity of payback over the UK leaving their club.

"There are also bodies of our people," Allen told her. Icing on the cake.

"I want them buried on our side of the border," she replied without hesitation.

"I can't imagine you'll meet any resistance," he smiled. "However, doing so will support any request from the Italians to have their fallen returned and possibly even a portion of the treasure."

"Do we have an estimate for the treasure found?"

"A rough estimate puts it at ten million. Priceless artefacts included. Apparently a tomb was hidden beneath one of the forts."

"Where were our people buried?"

"Outside the tomb's entrance. About thirty bodies piled high in a narrow grave."

"Get me the Italian President on the line followed by the Pope," she said.

***

When Bandip warned him, the Italian President was on the line he was surprised but quick to figure the reason for the call. Enrico De Lucca spoke fluent English with a crisp Italian accent.

"Rupert, I've learned that you have good news for me."

"Really, Enrico and where did you receive that information?"

The other man laughed, "No one gives up their sources Rupert. But tell me what has been found at Hadrian's Wall or should I say beneath it?"

"You have very good sources Enrico. We only discovered a tomb yesterday and it's still undergoing examination. It will take a few days before we really know what's been uncovered."

"You will understand that I will be hoping to receive the bodies of any Italians discovered returned home. Together with their possessions."

"As soon as I'm made fully aware of what's been found I'll let you know," he replied unwilling to be pinned down.

"I will pass your words on to the Pope," De Lucca added before ending the call.

Bandip joined him after the call using the seat in front of his desk to get comfortable. "He knows about the tomb."

"You can't keep something like that quiet, but I admit I expected at least another twenty-four hours before it reached Italy and the Pope. They're going to introduce religion into any argument."

"What do you want to do?"

"Return the bodies. Keep the treasure."

"Can we afford to do that?"

"You're thinking about the EU, but I'm not prepared to be bullied by them. The bodies and treasure were found in English territory. Damn it it's been there for two thousand years and would still be here if it hadn't been discovered!"

"You might have to negotiate and share it." Bandip told him.

"Balls!" He snapped. "We're keeping the lot. I'm not prepared to give anyone anything that's found here. Possession is nine tenths of the law. That's the law I follow and I'm not about to change. The treasure is ours including all artefacts. If anyone wants them they're going to have to buy them."

"What about the Scots?"

"What about them?"

"We believe some of their ancestors were also present. Does that mean they also have a right to a part of the treasure?"

"They were on our side of the Wall. The answer is no."

He nodded. No doubt Bonnie Burns would consider several feet of wall insufficient to deter a request to share the treasure. "Well, apart from this latest incident the reconstruction project is keeping to its time scales even with an increase in demonstrations by the Scots."

"I've only ever seen about fifty demonstrators at any one time."

"It's now around five hundred with tents. The longer and higher the wall gets the more likely it is the number of demonstrators will increase. Scottish police are dealing with them, but I've heard complaints about the cost of policing what is ostensibly an English barricade."

"Yet we have no demonstrators this side of the wall," he pointed out.

"Not yet," Bandip agreed. The notion that Scots living in England might join their brothers and sisters and begin demonstrating on the English side remained a distinct possibility. However, so far, the reconstruction appeared to carry the support of an English public accustomed to their historic structures being refurbished no matter the cost. Would the find of treasure change anything?

CHAPTER TWELVE

That Reporter Again

Investigative reporting is not for everyone. It requires determination, focus and patience as well as willingness to put oneself in harm's way. For those who manage to stick with it a discovery of improved instincts follows. Boris Daley was someone who stuck with the profession he had chosen many years earlier learning more about the behaviour people adopted than almost possible in any other profession.

It was night in the middle of the week, and he was parked on a motorcycle in Greyhound Road Fulham, a cul-de-sac. The street lighting offered dismal illumination that failed to penetrate the rain-soaked darkness further than a few feet from its pole. Close to the end of the cul-de-sac Lord Selwyn Horny sat in the back of his black Mercedes limousine alongside a less prestigious vehicle. The question in his mind. Why was someone like Horny having a clandestine meeting at night?

Daley sat there an hour before the other vehicle drove out of the cul-de-sac followed moments later by Horny. Catching both on his mobile camera he sent a message to Bandip. Asking that he check the registration of the second vehicle.

At home Bandip was alone when he received Daley's message. Without hesitation contacting the police while waiting online for an answer. The owner of the second vehicle, a Ford Focus, was Fawad Bai a Pakistani immigrant of ten years with a criminal record for petty crimes. When Bandip tried contacting Daley, he went straight to voice mail.

***

The following day he shared Daley's message with Streaker after another call with further information from the police.

"You're sure about this? You think there might be some kind of plan to threaten my family because we're disbanding the Lords." The Prime Minister asked, grim faced.

"The images Daley sent me clearly show both vehicles leaving moments after one another. Their meeting took place at eleven thirty and lasted an hour. Daley himself can't imagine why Horny would meet with a petty villain without there being a deeper meaning."

"You're suggesting that Bai's brother who heads a Croydon based human trafficking outfit should be considered a warning. But Horny's a Lord for heaven's sake. The man has status. To imagine him dealing with criminals to do my family harm as a way of forcing me to change my mind over the Lords is pushing my imagination to its limit."

"He hates to lose," Bandip replied unwilling to relax the pressure on his boss.

"I appreciate that you're looking after my interests Jonathon. I do, but what you're suggesting is difficult for me to get my head around. We really need more evidence. Hopefully, Daley will be able to find it provided it exists."

"The police are already monitoring the Bali family. Do you want me to request they do the same with Horny?"

"No," he replied firmly. His concern over any leak that police were keeping a prominent Lord under surveillance likely to create a firestorm from within his own Party. No matter what suspicions might be available to use as evidence. Besides many would argue that the evidence was circumstantial at best and mere coincidence at worst. Not that any believed in coincidence. "We keep this between ourselves for now. Give Daley whatever help he needs. Nothing more."

"What about your children?" Bandip asked.

He nodded. The police driver who daily took his children to school reported spotting the same vehicle behind them over three consecutive days. The fact that the driver used three different routes each time heightened his concern. The vehicle's registration returned an ownership record linked to a painting decorator firm in Croydon. "I can't believe Horny would be so stupid."

"He's incredibly arrogant and not someone to easily give-up power," Bandip reminded him. "There have been several incidents in his past that might have lost him his peerage. Abuse against women mostly. His first wife died in a motoring accident in which it was proved the brakes of her sportscar had been tampered. The culprit was never found. Horny himself was exonerated being in the U.S. at the time of her death. Looking at his background with a critical eye made the notion of Horny meeting with a known criminal less remarkable. The man has no shame and totally uninhibited to attain his goal. The fact you visited him at his private club to warn him off submitting contracts for the relocation project has circulated throughout the Lords. You've given him something to prove." He finished watching Streaker force himself to believe in something that defied belief.

"Our families go to the same church," Streaker snapped.

"You made an enemy of him when you decided to shut down the Lords. He's not alone, but if anyone is going to take action to stop you my money would be on him." Bandip refused to be stopped ignoring the irritation caused. A necessary pain.

"I intend discussing the matter with MI Three. In the meantime, I want a second police vehicle escorting my kids to and from school. Also, I don't want the police paying a visit to the painter decorator firm in Croydon at this stage. Let me discuss our concerns with MI Three and see what they have to offer."

Bandip rose from the seat, "Yes Rupert."

Left alone Streaker turned on his seat to stare out of the window. Immersed in disbelief that anyone so close in government would stoop to consider doing something against him through his children. If true he would show no quarter.

CHAPTER THIRTEEN

Northern Ireland & Wales

Meetings between political leaders in Wales were traditionally held at *ŷ Hywel* situated in Cardiff. The name of the building a historical reference to the medieval king Hywel Dda (circa 880-948). Previous to that it was known as Crickhowell House, the name derived from the former Secretary of State for Wales, Lord Crickhowell. The building itself opened in 1991 constructed of red brick with a corridor to the Senedd debating chamber in Cardiff Bay.

Today a meeting between the Northern Irish First Minister Lorraine Robertson and First Minister for Wales Donna Davies was discovered to possess minor communications issues. Whereas Davies spoke English with a slow methodology that overcame her crisp Welsh accent. Robertson unwittingly slipped back into a customary high-speed dialect accentuated by an Irish twang that only locals could untangle. To an onlooker it appeared as if she were talking fast before a thought was lost. Awareness that the conversation with her Welsh counterpart was adrift identified by a glazed expression staring back at her. Reigning back each time when her enthusiasm for the project they were discussing got away from her. Their discussion about a joint project to capture fresh water for export the first of its kind.

"Additional funding will prove a problem Donna."

Davies sighed, "Isn't it always but the potential returns speak for themselves. Even Rupert Streaker couldn't deny that!"

With similar backgrounds they recognized a shared intention to improve their separate economies as well as the necessity to bring both England and Scotland with them if they were to be successful.

"We need to lower the temperature between England and Scotland caused by the Hadrian's Wall project. It can only end in another independence referendum and a real possibility of a broken Kingdom. I believe our project has the ability to heal wounds and give hope through unity. I just hope the Prime Minister agrees." Robertson said, doing so slowly to avoid comprehension issues.

"Fresh water is a prevalent natural resources that remains untapped, pardon the pun," Davies smiled. "Initial costs are enormous but by spreading them to new constructions through mandatory legislation public funding can be reduced. The only stumbling block I envisage are water companies. Like their electric counterparts they'll block any efforts that reduces their profits."

"A good reason to nationalise water," Robertson said. The term unfamiliar to someone who usually opposed nationalization in line with her Party's policy. "My saying so demonstrates how far we've come. The world has changed, and we need to change with it. Making water a level playfield is a 'must' if we're to be successful Donna."

"No argument from me on that score Lorraine. We believe all critical human life sustenance should be nationalized including energy and transport."

"Don't let's go there while we're doing so well," Robertson smiled. "Question is how do we convince Rupert Streaker we're right?"

"He's changed," Davies said. "Since the relocation began I've noticed he's acting more like a centrist than a full-blown Tory. I'm pretty sure he'll at the very least listen to what we have to say rather than dismiss us from the outset."

"The knives are out over the Lords being made redundant. He might not consider his current position able to view our project fairly. I've heard that Lord Horny is kicking up trouble."

"That sod," Davies said with disdain. "I'll never forget he tried to grope me in his office then got upset after I fought him off. He doesn't like losing. Several from the Party refused to acknowledge me afterwards. It went on for a year before things improved."

"Vindictive bastard," Robertson said. "Never did like him either."

"To be fair to Streaker he has his hands full right now. What I'm hoping is that he'll view our proposal as a lifeline that deals with a problem we're all facing."

"By making a profit from it," Robertson added.

"Perhaps we should inform him that we've each committed to the project on a small scale as an exercise that will determine whether we continue?"

Robertson nodded, "But to be viable we need national legislation that make developers create home and industrial small-scale reservoirs. As well as having them ensure connections to the larger primary distribution centres if we're to run pipelines to ports as well as Scotland and Northern England. Installing the necessary legislation is fundamental to our purpose. That's where we need him onside."

"Perhaps we're thinking about approaching him when we should be thinking about approaching her. His wife. Jessica is an environmentalist who has been vocal over the devastation caused by flooding to the northern counties."

"Are you in a position to speak to her without him getting upset?"

"I see her at least once a month for coffee. We're friends. She's switched on as far as politics is concerned and knows who is doing what most of the time. I could get our conversation round to flooding and call her attention to our project."

Robertson smiled, "Donna, I think you may have a plan."

CHAPTER FOURTEEN

Enter Luna Broom

Luna Broom had been elected Mayor of London for less than six months and still growing accustomed to her new role as head of the executive of the Greater London Authority. Directly elected Mayors were introduced in 2000 her predecessors being much older than her tender 30 years. Something that attracted much consternation from the media, but so far without reason. The people voted for her and she was determined to do her best for them. Such a single-minded approach together with unprecedented transparency appeared to keep voters onside.

Had anyone asked her why she won the election for mayor she would have pointed to her Green credentials that had attracted environmentalists to rally to her. Yet a passion for astrology and the afterlife gave her opponents an arsenal of ammunition with which to criticize including Rupert Streaker who labelled her *Looney*

Broom. Yet nothing appeared to phase her supporters that they had chosen wisely.

Streaker had been a right-wing member of the Party displaying more than passing contempt for any who disagreed with his faction. Becoming Prime Minister with an overwhelming majority appeared to cement his position. However, recently Broom had noticed, as had many others, his movement towards a more centrist position. Whether it would prove a long-term intention or simply a passing whim before the next election only time would tell. Today, however, she had been summoned by Streaker. The reason behind his request a mystery.

Broom appeared her customary confident self. A pretty red head with freckled cheeks and generous lips. Green eyes that blended with a knee length green suit matching earrings and shoes. Her younger sister Venus had accompanied her as was their practice when attending potentially controversial meetings. Venus acting as her personal aide. The pair similar in looks except for blonde hair. At any other time, Streaker might have been attracted to either of them. She began the conversation without wasting time on preliminaries. Her dislike for Streaker obvious by her tone, "You asked me to visit Prime Minister."

"I did," Streaker replied. Most individuals in his position might have felt uncomfortable dealing with an opponent such as Broom. Particularly after giving her a cruel nickname. Ignoring their differences, a necessity that overcame all else. "I wanted to hear your opinion regarding the relocation of Parliament?"

"Isn't it a bit late for that," she asked eyebrows raised in curiosity. "I mean you've already gone ahead with it. If my math is correct you've been going ahead with it for the past eighteen months. Why ask me now?"

"Are you for or against it?" He persisted.

"It should come as no surprise to you. I'm for it," she told him a confused glance at her sister.

"Didn't see that question coming from reading the Tarot eh?" He chuckled. Her straight-faced expression denounced his humour as unworthy of the situation. While her sister remained totally indifferent. Continuing quickly on, "What about the change over to the Second Chamber instead of continuing the House of Lords?"

"Good riddance to the lot of them. It's well overdue."

"You realize that you might have been eligible to join the Lords yourself."

"Not interested."

"I appreciate that you're a new broom, pardon the pun, and want to change things but not everything needs changing. The old adage if it's not broke don't fix it applies."

"You lost me at broom," she retorted. "If I'm here simply for you to practice taking snipes at me this meeting is over!" She said both sisters rising from their seats.

"I didn't. Please sit down this is important. I'll try to curtail my diverse sense of humour." Something unfamiliar in his tone caught her attention. Almost a plea.

She did as he asked as did her sister.

"Good."

"Let's stop beating about the bush Rupert. You want something from me what is it?" Looney Broom was no fool he reminded himself. Making a mental note not to even think of her nickname. Especially now when he might need her support. A glance at her sister whose unmoving features remained a constant that gave no hint what she was thinking. Unnerving. "I've heard rumblings from a variety of quarters that opposition is growing."

"I'm sure you have. I know Jonathon Bandip is an excellent aide. Finding things out is what he does."

"But even he has limits," he told her.

Her eyes narrowed as she weighed up what she was likely to hear next, "I'm still at a loss why you thought to ask me for help?"

"Well, let's be honest you don't like me very much. Do you?"

"You can't blame me for that. You're the one who calls me a looney because I read the Tarot and follow astrology. What do you do in your personal time? Blood sports I imagine. You need to feel powerful and killing defenceless animals allows you that."

He sighed this was proving tougher than he imagined. Her sister still showed no sign of expression. Maybe she had died without them realizing, he thought. "The only animals I'm interested at this time are those found in the Lords. Now tell me what you think of Selwyn Horny?"

A whirlpool of seething filled her eyes, "I see what you're up to Rupert. You know that I detest Horny even more than I do you and you're hoping to secure my help in any future battle he might be bringing to your door."

"Well done Luna. You understand me perfectly." Leaning back on the seat it creaked unexpectedly.

"I can't help you," she said.

"Or won't?" He replied.

"Yes, that's it I won't," she said and rose from the seat a second time.

"Do you think him vindictive enough to go after my children?"

The fact that she returned her posterior to the seat told him she did not doubt such a possibility. "He's possibly one of the nastiest people I've ever encountered. I wouldn't put anything past him. What makes you ask such a question?" Genuine curiosity in her tone.

"At this time let me just say there have been too many coincidences where my children are concerned. Nothing sufficient for me to turn to the police but certainly sufficient to cause Jonathon and Bernice Walters to be concerned for their safety."

"I see," she said. "What exactly are you asking of me?"

"He wouldn't be doing anything alone. Someone or maybe more than one person in the Commons is helping him. I need to know who. As London Mayor you have a useful financial network at your disposal. We need to follow the money to discover who is backing Horny."

"On one condition," she said abruptly. "You make a formal apology over the nickname you labelled me with."

Which one, he thought momentarily. "Of course."

"It was highly unprofessional and not something that should enter the head of an adult."

"I was probably having a bad day."

"Well, you can apologize in one of your friend's nationals. Call in Bernice and Jonathon I want them to witness this. I also want her to record the statement you will have printed."

With his aide and secretary present Broom repeated what she considered a reasonable apology for print in a national daily of Streaker's choice.

"After I've seen it in print I'll do what I can," with that she and her sister left them.

"Sounds like a book rather than an article covering an apology," he said. "Ask the lawyers to check it over for me before it goes to print. Also, Jonathon add something at the end that makes me look less like a ten-year-old."

"What did her sister have to say?"

"Absolutely nothing. Just sat there staring at me. Quite creepy," he said. "Can't imagine anything worse."

"She could have arrived with both sisters," he said.

"Good grief, you mean there's three of them. Is her name derived from some planet too?"

"Andromeda," Bandip smiled.

"I knew it. Are there any more siblings?"

"A brother," he replied.

"What name did they lumber him with?"

"Pluto."

"Poor bloke."

"Is it really necessary to go ahead with this apology?" He asked.

"It is if I want her help to beat Horny. Just get it done."

CHAPTER FIFTEEN

Fate

It was dark as Selwyn Horny raced home in his Range Rover beneath an unrelenting rainstorm. Hitting ninety miles an hour along the A18 between Laceby and Ludborough in Lincolnshire. A road infamous as Britain's deadliest. Ignoring speed cameras Horny was in a hurry to return to the snug comfort of his country estate after a day spent at Westminster.

Ahead of him hidden behind a veil of rain and shadow a broken-down forty tonne heavy goods vehicle occupied most of the carriageway. The five-axle behemoth's seized gearbox locked. Electrics without power. The driver in its cab waiting for rescue. Horny didn't see it until too late. The Range Rover's headlights picking out its outline giving no time to avoid. The inevitable collision deafening momentarily drowning out the heavy downpour.

Its driver felt the huge lorry shudder and glanced at a wide-angle side mirror. A single headlight on the Land Rover still glowed after the crash lighting up the giant rear wheels under the trailer he was hauling.

***

Next day Bandip informed Streaker of the accident.

"How he survived is a miracle," Bandip began. "Suffering a fractured skull, broken jaw, collar bone and right arm. Broken left leg and right ankle. Broken ribs. The list seems to go on and on. Apparently he's covered from head to toe in plaster and bandages."

"I want to visit him," Streaker said. An impulsive notion grabbing him.

"Do you think that wise?" He asked uncertainly.

"Very. Make the arrangements."

***

Streaker arrived at the Lincoln County hospital the following day. Determined to avoid meeting a press barrage his clandestine visit included only senior members of the hospital staff. His security retinue kept to a minimum.

Horny was almost totally covered in bandages and plaster. Stretched out on a bed with one leg lifted on a winch. Asking to be left alone he stood alongside the bed and saw his rivals eyes focus on his appearance between layers of bandage. If they could speak abuse would have filled the air. Hatred was something Horny had mastered. Eyes, facial expressions, and body language and those before he even opened his mouth.

"Seems you've had a spot of bad luck Selwyn." He said with an unrestrained smile.

"Ugh." All Horny could muster in reply.

"I wanted you to know. I discovered that you were intending to go after my family. You're a very vindictive arse and quite stupid for thinking that you could get away with such a thing."

Silence. Eyes narrowing full of menace.

"It would have been a mistake had you done so. You understand that don't you. Because I wouldn't have stopped until I destroyed you. There would have been nowhere to hide no one to turn to for help."

Silence.

"You shouldn't feel too bad about the accident. They tell me that you should fully recover after six months. By which time you will have had time to reconsider. Time to understand just how awful your life could really be if you'd made one vindictive mistake too many."

"Ugh," he grunted. Eyes more relaxed.

"On the bright side you're saving the taxpayer around thirty-eight thousand pounds by not receiving the Lords attendance allowance for so long. I'm sure they would thank you for that."

"Ugh, ugh!" he growled angrily.

"You've always been a tight-fisted sod even though you're worth a damn sight more than me! The House of Lords is finished. Get over it."

"Ugh, aaghh," he grumbled. The last part of his response a sign of pain as his jaw tried to move.

"I thought it best for me to come all this way to have a quiet chat. Just so that we understand each other. Good luck with the recovery." Turning away with that refreshing feeling that makes a long journey worthwhile he returned to his car.

CHAPTER SIXTEEN

A meeting of minds

The visit to the relocation site had been coordinated by Number 10. It was a special moment in the enterprise with the completion of the circular half mile diameter building platform completed. Fifty feet above the land it provided an unprecedented view of all round it. Constructed from a modern sophisticated concrete with a self-repair capability that stems from a form of the Bacillus bacteria.. In the event of cracks, limestone is produced, and the cracks sealed. The bacteria has a dormant lifespan of 200 years making it a long-term answer.

Thirty feet below the top platform a second smaller maintenance podium was sited. A third the size of its big higher brother it was already occupied by maintenance buildings being readied for the project manager Bernard Allfores to leave his humble mobile office on the ground.

Today was a special day for the Relocation Project with the completion of the top platform, now officially referred to as Pier Two. Additionally, four circular pads equally distanced from each other surrounded Pier Two standing forty feet high. Ten feet lower to create a sense of majesty of the new Parliament buildings. The pads intended to cater for Sky Train, Helipads, buses coaches and a limited number of private vehicles. Pedestrian access from each via two-hundred-foot-long enclosed bridges. Even without the construction of the central buildings the platforms looked impressive. A small delegation of politicians and local councillors from London and Blackburn arrived to attend the official opening of Pier Two.

Allfores had never believed in love at first sight. A married man in his forties should have been passed that sort of thing. The moment he caught sight of Luna Broom his heart missed a beat and the breath knocked out of him as if stomach punched. Gliding towards him the others with her blurred to insignificance. Only his delayed greeting finally catching their attention.

"Are you alright Mister Allfores?" She asked now in front of him. Small by comparison.

"I... Yes, I'm sorry. Welcome to the Relocation Project." At last, finding his voice.

"I was flattered that Number Ten invited me to preview the opening of the central platform and to meet with you. I've heard and read so many good things about what you've been able to achieve."

"You're being kind," he replied, head still reeling. Not yet able to meet her direct gaze. "There are as many bad things said about me as good."

"But the figures do not lie and neither does this enormous platform," she retorted. "It really is a marvel of engineering as worthy as the buildings created by Augustus Pugin and Charles Barry back in the nineteenth century. Barry was in his forties also."

"You flatter me too much Mayor. I'm not the architect merely the project leader."

"But wasn't it you who wanted the new building sited on a platform to avoid flooding?"

"Yes, but…"

"And haven't you been responsible for the draft design ideas of a vision you yourself hold?"

"I suppose so, but…"

"You're far too modest Bernard.. do you mind if I call you Bernard?"

"Not at all…"

"Please call me Luna. Everyone does. Mayor makes me sound like some old frump." She paused momentarily studying him catching his shy gaze.

"You also brought about the recent proposal for a Skytrain. I so love that idea."

"Thank you."

"You need to tell people what you've achieved otherwise those honours will be taken by others less worthy. Put your stamp on them so people will always remember who to thank for this fantastic building and its transport network. You've almost singlehandedly changed the dynamics of this nation's will to split."

"I think some recognition for that enormous achievement should be directed at the Prime Minister. After all it was his initial vision that I'm fulfilling."

She turned away to face the small crowd behind them. Jonathon Bandip there too as the nominal Number 10 representative. "Please give us a moment for a private chat." Her two sister and brother accustomed to her unorthodox qualities immediately turned on the small crowd of six or seven public servants including Bandip. Leading them away.

"I didn't expect to reach this conversation quite so soon," she said when out of earshot. "Why did Rupert Streaker choose you for this job when he had so many of his chums champing at the bit for it?"

"You'll have not ask him. All I can say is that I hope I'm proving worthy of his choice."

Her sympathetic smile enough to reveal understanding, "Loyalty is a highly prized trait in the political arena. He certainly has it where you're concerned. I don't understand why you would join with him given your history?"

There it was he thought. His wife. The lurid photograph of her with Streaker having sex on a church altar. Everyone wanted to know, even apparently the woman who just bowled him over without knowing it. "is that what this is really all about. You just want some gossip to take back to London that you can snigger over for a few months?"

Had it been true she would have slapped his face and stormed off. "I want to know because I sense one of you is getting a raw deal and Streaker isn't the kind to accept such a thing. He recently asked for my help over a personal issue that suddenly resolved itself. My payment was for him to apologise in the national press for nicknaming me 'Looney Broom'". Ordinarily I would have told him to shove it where the Sun don't shine but an apology like that easily outweighed my reluctance to help. I just wanted to know if you'd experienced something similar?"

Her honesty he did not doubt. Yet to disclose the details of his pact with Streaker would cost him his job and who knew what else. "He can't do much to the Mayor of London. You're elected. My situation is different. I enjoy my work and intend seeing it through to the end."

"I understand," she smiled. "You have sad eyes."

Her last words caught him off guard, "I'm sorry?"

"You look sad," she said.

An urge to talk about his wretched personal life caught on the tip of his tongue. "Are any of us truly happy?"

"You probably won't believe this but there are times in life when we meet someone who we feel we've encountered before, but not in this reality. Someone with whom we automatically feel drawn towards as though an old friend. That's what I felt when I first saw you."

Not knowing what to say was becoming a problem for him. She shared similar feelings he had in regards their first encounter. Perhaps not as strong or heartfelt, but she acknowledged a sense of their having met before. Not that they had. At least not in this lifetime. Of that he was certain. As certain as he was that she was not someone he would ever have forgotten. "I read that you're interested in astrology, the mystic arts."

"Yes, does that turn you off?" A hint of defensive defiance in her tone made him relax.

"Not at all. Though you'd find me boring in the extreme. I'm very focused on work and rarely delve into my spirituality."

"Pity. I sense you have great depth in that department," she replied.

"I'd like to invite you to dinner to continue our conversation, but I'm sure you're intending to return to London tonight. Perhaps we could do so another time."

"I'm here overnight and would be delighted. Now we better get back to the others before we become the latest news item."

Watching them from a distance Bandip used his mobile to take a snapshot of their close conversation. Intimacy obvious.

***

While Allfores and the Mayor arranged dinner plans Kate Allfores was on the move through Westminster Hall, a part of the Palace of Westminster built in 1097. With eyes gazing up she mused over the kings and queens who had travelled the same route. Marvelling at the hammerbeam roof architecture, possibly the greatest feat of medieval architecture of the period. Allowing the original three aisles beneath to be turned into a single huge open space thereby creating the largest hall in all Europe at the time. During the reign of King Richard II so much changed including the erection of fifteen life-sized statues of kings erected in recesses that stretched from end to end. Their existence immortalized. She found it easy to lose herself in the splendour of such history. Losing sight of the people moving busily back and forth around her until she came to an abrupt halt with a bump.

"Sorry," she said turning her attention to the figure beside her.

"My fault," Streaker said before realizing who he had encountered.

At an immediate loss for words as they stared at the other.

"Fancy meeting you here Rupert," she finally said.

"Yes," he grinned. "Of all places. It's been so long…"

"More than eighteen months. Not that I'm counting."

"I'm sorry," he began.

Raising a hand, she stopped him. "I understand, always have done. You've a career, wife, and children. Our fling couldn't compete with that. Not matter how enjoyable it was."

"How's Bernard?" He asked glancing at passers-by. Some purposely avoiding eye contact. Everyone knew the scandal. Very few the truth.

She chuckled. No humour in it. "It finished. The minute he found out the truth. He's a very upright citizen. Loyal to a fault and expects the same in return. I failed him. We're separated and our divorce is going through."

"Are you seeing anyone?"

Her smile gave away what she was thinking. He was searching for an easy way out of an awkward situation. By claiming a new boyfriend, she would give him a reason to feel less guilty. That she had several none of his business. "No one special."

"I was asking because you're a beautiful woman and the idea of you being alone for eighteen months seems impossible." He still found her attractive. Sexy. In fact, she remained the sexiest woman he had ever met. One lusted after since schooldays even when she was later just another notch on a long list of conquests. It wasn't something easily explained. How or why an individual possessed that kind of irresistible power over another, but for him she had it in spades. Even now he could feel himself stirring with desire.

"I know I never told you this before Rupert, but I never enjoyed sex with anyone else as much as with you. I guess knowing that dimmed my expectations with other men. I just can't be bothered going through the motions anymore." Her lie came easily. He had thrown her under the bus when his career was threatened by scandal. Emerging the victim of a nasty conspiracy against his premiership rather than a cheating husband. Gaining public support against media infringement of privacy to smear political leaders. While he extricated himself from the scandal she came to symbolize the dangers for men from women who slept around to better themselves. As his celebrity status rose her flatlined. Did she hate him for it?

He wasn't certain but what she said sounded like an indirect invitation. "It's the same for me."

"Are you just saying that to be polite?" Her smile brightened.

"I've no reason to lie," he said holding her gaze. Uncertain about his own motives. Whether he was behaving towards her as he did any woman. Flirting just to find out whether he was in with a chance.

"Rupert, I do believe you're being honest," her smiled remained.

"Your instincts still work well Kate."

"Does that mean I still interest you?"

He sniffed the air looked around at people passing by. None able to hear their conversation. "You and I have a connection Kate. Whether it's a previous life connection or simply a chemical reaction. We do one thing really well together and you know precisely what that is."

"Even better than Jessica?" She asked, eyes full of mischief. If only she had recorded their conversation she thought to herself. Without hesitation she continued, "You still want to shag me."

His expression became serious, "I'm not dead and you're till gorgeous." He refused to be drawn into comparisons that could be used later. Jessica could destroy his ambitions overnight. Talking to Kate Allfores suddenly suppressing his libido. What it was that turned him on flirting with dangerous women an unknown. It did but it needed to stop as far as Kate was concerned. There could never be any doubt that she remained the most toxic of his lovers.

She chuckled, "Staying stum with that one. Clever boy."

"By the way how's the relocation project going?" He asked, catching himself before he slipped too far.

"As well as you might have hoped," she replied, understanding what he was about. "There are several tenders from foreign corporations wanting to purchase all of the buildings. This hall for instance. I've received a five-billion-pound offer from a Russian mogul."

"And what does he want to do with it?"

"Turn it into an exclusive conference forum for the leaders of Asian countries. He sees it as giving them a chance to sample English hospitality and its environment while at work."

"And the return on his five billion quid investment will be what?"

"Mega," she replied. "Each country will donate X amount per annum if it wants to be represented here. To miss out will not go well for any who aren't represented."

"I look forward to reading his proposal."

"It was nice seeing you again Rupert," she said.

"Take care of yourself. Keep up the good work." He couldn't believe he had just said that and gave himself a mental kick for stupidity.

As she moved away he glanced round at the people passing some now willing to meet his gaze and nod. No doubt their brief encounter would be reported to Jessica. Fortunately, nothing happened, and he needed to ensure it never did. Tough when possessed with the libido of a jack rabbit.

***

It was late evening by the time Streaker returned to his residential accommodation at Number 10. The children were in bed and his wife sat curled up on a sofa in the lounge reading a magazine. Looking up as he appeared, "That was a long day."

"Why is it they all feel that way," he chortled moving over to a drinks cabinet to pour himself a neat whiskey. "Want one?"

"No thanks."

He joined her on the sofa after removing his jacket and tie whiskey in hand. "And what about your day?"

Her gaze returned to the magazine, "Quite fruitful. I met with Donna Davies today."

His right eyebrow rose a half inch. Well aware that the First Minister for Wales used their friendship as a conduit to him. "And what revelations did Donna have to inspire us with today?"

"I don't believe that you're aware she and Lorraine Robertson are cooking up an economic project together." There it was. His wife working for him in plain sight. Furnishing him with information that revealed the intentions of others. "They're intending to approach you about exporting fresh water to arid regions around the world and I think they may have a point."

"Sounds expensive," he replied almost dismissively.

"They knew you'd say that." She replied quickly adding. "It's why they want to initially trial their theory and are hoping that you'll support them."

"What exactly does trial their theory mean in real terms?"

"Long-term, it means pipelines. The trial will require half a dozen tankers to prove there's a demand and that it's willing to pay and make the UK a profit."

"Alright, so far so good. What's the catch?"

"The introduction of some legislative mumbo jumbo that makes it mandatory for all new construction, home and industry to be equipped with water reservoir systems. The creation of a freshwater channelling system that follows the canal system across the country to reduce infrastructure costs."

Yet again he thanked the Victorians. With a nationwide canal network of almost 4,000 miles their foresight and inventiveness brought about a dynamic change that aided the effectiveness of the industrial revolution. Creating wealth through industry ultimately leading to the rise of the British Empire during the Victorian era. The use of canals to transport raw materials to manufacturers and on to consumers reduced time and costs while making use of an overground channel. "You sound supportive?"

"I don't deny the idea of selling our rainwater to dry countries in the Middle East and elsewhere appealing."

"Provided profits make such a venture worthwhile," he reminded her. "They've costed against the latest desalination plants. Needless to say, pipelines are cheaper. By proving selling fresh water from shipping tankers returns a profit they hope to convince Government it's a worthwhile venture. Not only that but in regions where flooding is an issue the introduction of millions of small reservoirs pipelined to several distribution points on the coast allows the disposal of fresh water for a commercial purpose while removing the flooding threat."

"Who do we get from the commercial sector to invest in this project?"

"Insurance companies," she replied simply. "Their investors not only get a return by accepting insurance cover for those living in previously threat flooded regions. The fresh water sold to other countries gives them a second return on their investment. It's literally a win-win."

Streaker could feel her enthusiasm reach across. Not something he could or should ignore. Her intuition always reliable. Her focus being for the good of his career undisputed. She was the perfect partner. Any threat to their relationship viewed in his own mind as a shot in the foot. Comparisons between her and Kate Allfores repeatedly failed to inspire a similar confidence in the latter. Jessica was loyal to a fault the same could not be said of Kate Allfores. In that moment he decided not to speak to Kate and definitely not to meet. "Okay, I'll look at their proposal. You can tell Donna your fishing trip was successful."

She leaned forward and kissed him.

"Shag!" Behind them Pecker the parrot squawked.

Streaker shrugged, "Maybe he's right."

"Shag!" Dolly the second parrot squawked.

"Shag!" A third parrot squawked.

Streaker spun round, "Three birds!"

Jessica smiled oblivious of the shock in his eyes, "I forgot to tell you. Her name's Belle. She's homeless."

"She's here," he pointed out. "Hardly homeless."

"She was homeless until I stepped in," looking at him faces close her scent flooded his nostrils. "You don't mind darling, do you?"

Staring at the three birds each on their separate perch he wished he could say something stronger. Something that revealed he didn't like parrots, especially ones that repeatedly squawked 'shag'. Instead, he nodded smiled and shrugged like it was no problem. It made her happy and he wanted her happy with him if he expected her to help him. A small sacrifice if she helped him reach his goal of a public statue outside the new Parliament buildings. As they headed out of the lounge the three parrots squawked 'shag' one at a time. The word loud as it followed them to their bedroom.

CHAPTER SEVENTEEN

Unity

The meeting of the three First Ministers and Streaker was claimed by Number 10 as an assembly of UK leadership that would bring unity where there was division. The rebuild of Hadrian's Wall considered an insult by the Scots generating resentment towards Westminster growing by the day. Since 2000 too many *'Establishment figures'* had been vocally hyper-critical of the Scottish drive for independence ignoring the harm it might do. Added to unfamiliar environment heaped on them by Brexit and the deathly COVID pandemic the winds of change were taking hold. Opinions swayed by Bonnie Burns and the Scottish National Party (SNP) leadership that Scotland could stand alone and would be better off for doing so began to appear feasible.

Westminster was its own worst enemy. Populated by arrogant overindulgent families that presented badly to those they represented it was clear something needed to be done if the union was to be saved. Number 10's formidable propaganda machine had been hard at work two weeks before the meeting declaring new strategies to improve the economy were under discussion and a favourable outcome expected to be reported after the meeting. To ensure a positive outcome Streaker had gone to get lengths to keep secret another possible project likely to greatly improve the environment. Something that would undoubtedly prove controversial yet merited consideration. Known as someone who never sat at a negotiating table a contingency plan. He was comfortable that should the freshwater export project put forward by Northern Ireland and Wales not cement their joint futures his contingency would certainly stir interest. Additionally, he had proven even more secretive over the identity of the individual he had chosen to lead the co-ordination of joint projects from Number 10. An identity not even Bandip was aware. Something the aide found irritating.

Streaker's choice was Izzi Goeng an internationally famous public relations consultant educated in England at a university of note with twenty-five years' experience building an enviable reputation for creating unity through industry. Born of Italian Australian aboriginal parents he was unique. A one off with the eloquence, charm and intelligence expected from a leader in his field. At six foot five and weighing more than two hundred and thirty pounds provided him a conspicuous physical presence. While a bold handsome bone structure and dark swarthy complexion hinted at his aboriginal ancestry also proving exceedingly effective at winning over the opposite sex. He and Streaker had been friends since university and the opportunity to work alongside him managing one of the richest countries in the world was a dream come true. However, when something appears as good as Izzi Goeng predictably people wonder if he is too good to be true. Inevitably there's a dark side and in Goeng's case a very dark one at that.

Seated in the Cabinet room the four leaders faced each other, their aides alongside after a warm welcome Streaker began discussions.

"What are your thoughts on the proposal from NI and Wales Bonnie?"

Bonnie Burns First Minister for Scotland looked round at the others before speaking. Donna Davies for Wales and Lorraine Robertson for Northern Ireland.

"For it to be effective we need a network of pipelines that reach the driest regions. The initial investment would be high, but time would be on our side as the climate continues to increase the heat in those regions. Additionally, action to reduce flooding is a priority for all of us."

"Do you envisage problems with all new constructs both commercial and residential including a freshwater reservoir that links to a distribution point?"

"Clearly industrial sites will accommodate larger reservoirs but there will need to be some kind of scale agreement where residential properties are concerned. We might need to discuss that with local councils but at this time we haven't identified any issues of concern. However, I'll wait until we see the draft legislation to make it mandatory." She hesitated momentarily before adding, "It is however, clear that financial savings are possible if the rebuild of Hadrian's Wall were postponed."

It was not unexpected. The wall was proving an issue the Scots appeared determined to thwart. Perhaps they really were considering an invasion?

"The wall is an investment for the future. The figures show it will likely take just five years to recover costs from tourism and from then on we're in profit at least for the next hundred years."

"Not everything is about money," Burns told him. "The wall is seen by the Scottish people as a statement of contempt aimed at them from Westminster."

"Well, that's just daft Bonnie. It's no such thing and money is paramount at this time whether any of us like it or not. We're sowing the seeds for the future of our countries and families. To ignore the significance of the income we're likely to see as a result of rebuilding the wall would be ridiculous. Please assure your people that our intention is purely financial and has nothing whatever to do with emotions whatever they may be at Westminster. Also, I very much doubt any contempt even exists. Westminster wants a United Kingdom and is willing make that happen by investing in whatever's necessary to secure funding that create jobs, especially in the north."

She knew he was lying. What his mouth said didn't register with what his eyes were telling her, but instinct is not something any politician can use as an argument. "I'll try Rupert, but I still wish you would give it serious consideration if a need to delay the rebuild will help with funding more likely to benefit us all such as this freshwater project."

With a reluctant agreement from the Scots, he revealed an undisclosed part of his plan. "With a rise in the number of new projects either in play or under consideration I'm certain you'll all agree that we need a co-ordinator to monitor what's going on. If for no other reason than to identify when projects cross one another or offer an opportunity to reduce costs by being integrated in some regions."

"You have someone in mind?" Burns asked but it sounded more like a statement than question.

Pressing a button on his mobile before answering brought a knock at the door followed by the huge appearance of Izzi Goeng. A place at the table ready for him. Unsurprisingly he knew in which direction to move before sitting down elbows resting on the table broad friendly smile filling his handsome features.

"I'm sure Izzi Goeng is familiar to you all. He's accepted to act as project co-ordinator and will head a team of three here in Westminster before moving to the relocation at Blackburn."

"Welcome Izzi," Robertson said warming to his inimitable good looks. "How do you see the role you're taking on with four of us in the driver's seat?"

"Challenging," he grinned. "But I'm certain we will all work well together because we share the same motivations wanting the projects to prove successful. Rupert is correct when he claims that we're here to sow the seeds for the future. Choosing me to help is an honour."

"And why do you believe the British Government chose to hire you rather than find someone in-house thereby immediately saving what I imagine is a very high salary?" Burns asked with customary directness.

"My understanding," he replied unphased. Tone neutral. "Is that I was selected because of my international track record. Rupert wanted the very best no matter the expense. If I don't prove myself within the initial six months I'll be out on my ear."

"You seem concerned Bonnie?" Streaker asked maintaining calm.

"You used a newly promoted civil servant in Bernard Allfores for the Relocation Project and saved enormously as a consequence. I'm a little confused why after proving that our much lower paid civil servants are enormously capable of achieving success with complex projects that you found it necessary to hire a very expensive consultant with limited experience working within our government. To take on a project comparable to one you handed Allfores?"

"I disagree with you that the Co-ordination Project is comparable to the Relocation Project. It is much more than that by virtue of having to learn about several different projects to identify where interoperability may be adopted to generate efficiency savings. Bernard Allfores has indeed surpassed all expectations but I'm sure that even he would view the Co-ordination Project as one that needed more expertise than he currently has to offer." He paused to check the expressions of the others before adding. "Izzi may appear on the surface to be a considerable expense but in the long-term he's as much an investment as the projects themselves."

"How much is your salary Izzi?" Burns asked plainly.

"One million pounds per annum," he replied. "I'm undercutting all rivals because of my friendship with Rupert."

"To say that we'll be monitoring your progress with keen interest would be an understatement," she said. "Our best civil servant who is doing a remarkably good job with the Relocation Project is paid seventy thousands pounds per annum. Understandably, many of us were hopeful that Rupert, your friend, was beginning a fresh strategy for his political party by using workforce resources more readily available and cheaper than external consultants. Clearly that is not the case."

"If you do not mind my saying so First Minister," Goeng started. "I believe you do him a disservice. The Co-ordination Project will prove highly complex and if given to a civil servant will place them under unbearable pressure with little reward. In my experience over the past twenty-five years that has never been a good strategy to approach a single large-scale project let alone multiple ones if you truly want a successful outcome."

Burns fell silent. Point made.

Goeng too fell quiet. Comfortable that his argument had prevailed. The expressions of all others around the table confirming his win.

Bandip shifted uneasily on his seat. Not that anyone noticed they were too enamoured by Goeng. Something about the big man had never sat right with him since their first meeting ten years ago in Sierra Leone. His appearance had changed little since that time a few more wrinkles around the eyes and strands of grey in his hair, but nothing that stood out to reveal how long ago their introduction had been. Initially he had also been captivated by the dark steely eyes and friendly smile. The thick heavy tone that spoke perfect English. Everything about him had been perfect. Too perfect. Inwardly he gave Bandip the creeps. As if he should never drop his guard. Life was about to get a whole lot harder. That much he was certain.

Almost as the meeting appeared ready to conclude Streaker raised a controversial issue. "I would like you to all consider an environmental matter that is unlikely to go down well with much of the public but which I believe needs addressing." Meetings that are overlong inevitably lose the full attention of those involved by signalling the possibility of a negative public reaction he invigorated interest. "I'm proposing that by Twenty Thirty each household be permitted only two fossil fuelled vehicles but as many electric ones as they like. Taking such a radical step will no doubt infringe on people's rights to live as they want, but in the interests of the environment I believe it necessary for us to force down the number of fossil fuelled vehicles on our roads. Bringing in legislation that makes mandatory limited ownership of fossil fuelled vehicles per household is taking a leap ahead of every other nation. Leading the way by demonstrating what's needed to protect our planet."

There was a moment of complete silence as the others digested the proposal. "Why did you leave it until now to discuss?" Burns asked. Suspicious that he was pursuing some undisclosed financial interest in electric vehicles (EV). After more than a decade of witnessing profiteering by 'chums' of Tory Ministers now impossible to ignore the possibility.

"We put together a paper for you all to review that's been sent to your mailboxes. It will cause disquiet among the motoring communities, but I believe you will agree that the reduction in toxicity is well worth it."

"Very noble I'm sure," she replied. "However, such action will have a hugely detrimental impact on those living in rural areas who depend on fossil fuelled vehicles. Additionally, until the infrastructure is up and running to provide electric power for vehicles across the nation your proposal should remain an unfulfilled ambition."

"I agree," Robertson added. "However, we will still look at your proposal in the hope of juggling the number of vehicles to suit different areas."

"By that do you mean limit city regions to two fossil fuelled vehicles per household while all rural areas remain unchanged?" Davies asked.

"It would make sense," Streaker added. "That way we would be resetting the motorist mindset gradually rather than in one swift blast of legislation." He smiled, "The fact that you've just suggested something new for this proposal gives me hope that we'll be able to find a joint solution. However, whatever we decide we must demonstrate consistency across the entire country and make the introduction of any measures on one set date. With the four nations agreeing a policy taking identical steps to introduce and police it the public will be more appreciative of how much consideration has gone into it. Our unity is as important to the planet as the proposal itself. Please let me know your feelings by the end of May."

"I want to know where you stand on the treasure discovered at Hadrian's Wall," Burns began. "Are you going to share it with Scotland?"

"I'm not sure this is the appropriate meeting for such a discussion Bonnie," he said, hoping she would take the hint.

"I think it's a very appropriate meeting for us to discuss what has been found. My understanding is that you've refused any Italian claim of the treasure. Does that mean you don't intend to share it with us as well?"

"It was found on the English side of the wall. Had it been found on the Scots side we would have accepted the treasure is yours. However, as things stand it is ours. I'm not giving away what belongs to the England as you wouldn't give away what belongs to Scotland. Are you really going to argue this?"

She smiled, "No. I just wanted to hear where you stood."

Streaker studied her. Had she really just yielded to him. It was unusual. Yet that's exactly what she had done in front of witnesses. It was impossible for him not to wonder if she intended further conflict later. At least he had emphatically denied any treasure be passed to the Italians that had included a short conversation with the Pope explaining his reasons.

While the others mixed with one another over teas coffee and sandwiches wheeled into the room by catering staff Streaker was feeling exuberant. Excited that the meeting had gone better than anticipated. The First Ministers had gone along with almost every issue raised, no matter how reluctantly. They were for the first time in a long while finally working together. The Union safe for a little longer. He needed to celebrate. Needed sex. Not the routine kind with Jessica. Rather something that gratified his inner animal. Exiting the room after giving Bandip instructions to cover for him he returned to his office and called a paid for associate used whenever the need arose.

"I'll be there in thirty minutes be ready." He said the young woman's voice on the other end full of sexual nuance. His friend Granger Shallow had given him her contact number some years ago. As a contingency should the need for sexual gratification reach beyond the loving arms of his wife.

Using a non-descript Jaguar driven by his regular driver Tom Speed got him to his appoint within the thirty-minute estimate. The apartment in Belgravia located on the third floor of a six-floor building dating back one hundred years. Was situated close to the Harvey Nichols flagship department store. Leaving his bodyguard by the elevator he headed towards an apartment located at the end of the corridor. The floor tiled in white and black marble squares dulled the sound of footsteps as he approached the door and used knuckles against it for attention. It opened immediately as if the young woman inside were waiting close by.

Without invitation he stepped inside and the door closed behind him. A carpeted hallway stretched out ahead as he dropped jacket trousers and pants around his ankles. Member proudly rigid. Ready for action. The young woman a late twenties blonde wore a white housecoat that she slipped off revealing a very shapely nude form. Unmoving he feasted eyes on every curvaceous piece of bare flesh. Knowing much of it was artificial did nothing to dilute his enjoyment. Breast enlargements had created a tantalising spherical combination that defied gravity while buttocks had also undergone similar treatment. Yet it was her mouth that most held his attention. Rich yielding lips that reflected the chemical Botox used to relax muscles around them creating an exaggerated pout.

Launching himself at her expected. As was the urgent way he mauled and fondled. The urgency of his need causing him to puff her name, "Bambi!"

She gasped aloud, "Thumper."

"Bambi," he repeated thrusting hard.

"Thumper," she gasped again.

"Bambi."

"Thumper."

"Aaghh!" He groaned.

"Ooohhh," she moaned.

He finished.

Later that same evening and £2,000 less wealthy he returned to the hallway and bodyguard. A high price to secure her silence. His wife at Number 10 waiting for him unaware that tonight he would be too tired for further physical exercise.

The bodyguard, Bruce Blister watched his approach. Knowing that Streaker played around not something that he ever allowed to bother him. With more than ten years working in the personal protection of VIPs he took whatever VIPs revealed about themselves with a pinch of salt. Personal protection officers in the Metropolitan Police were not hired to be judgemental just to protect whoever they were assigned. The fact that he liked Jessica Streaker made it a little tougher, but breaking his silence would cause him so much flak together with the loss of his job that ultimately his silence was assured.

***

It was nine in the evening when he returned home and found Jessica waiting for him in the lounge. "Where were you?"

Her question ringed with suspicion. Any naivety regarding her husband's fidelity lost long ago. Pain at the idea that he had a basic need to stray with other women something she had already come to terms. She loved him. They had children. Discrete infidelity that she could not prove even with good reason for suspicion would not justify their break-up. Kate Allfores an alleged sexual partner caused them to come close to divorce. Avoided by publicly discrediting the accusation saved their marriage. She sometimes wondered if it were inevitable that eventually their marriage would end over his infidelities. Perhaps, but not without her doing all she could to keep them together. Like her husband she hated to lose. Abhorred that her family would say 'told-you-so'. Warning her against their marriage had continued up to their wedding day. Ignoring them had created rifts where none had previously existed especially with her father who openly disliked Streaker. Being wrong about the man she loved unthinkable then, less so now. Somehow her love continued. Suspicion fuelled by rumours of infidelity insufficient to alter her feelings. She had been made aware that he had been seen talking to Kate Allfores in the hall at Westminster. Out in the open for all to see. She had spent time thinking long and hard about their very public encounter. Not something anyone would do seeking discretion. For that reason, she had compartmentalized it out of out of sight and mind. Returning home late without an obvious excuse now raised fears that his relationship with Kate Allfores was resurrected.

"I needed to attend to something with a contact," he replied without hesitation. It was not a lie and came out smoothly.

"Who?" She persisted.

Pouring himself a whiskey a frown creasing his features, "Am I being interrogated?"

"I know you met Kate Allfores at Westminster recently. Did you meet with her tonight too?" Her heart in her mouth as she asked the question watching his reaction.

"We unexpectedly ran into each other. I've managed to dodge her for the last eighteen months even though she's working for me. It was inevitable we would come across one another eventually. You can't seriously believe we're involved?"

"Why shouldn't I?"

"First off, because I love you and our children," he said sipping at the drink before joining her on the sofa. "I'm not having an affair with Kate Allfores. I haven't been with Kate Allfores today."

"Who have you been with?"

"Bear Beddia," he replied tone cool, unnervingly calm. Reaching inside his jacket he took out a mobile and handed it to her. "He's on speed dial you can check."

Bear Beddia the newspaper magnate was already warned he might be used as an alibi. She made the call. Their conversation lasted no more than a minute. Returning the mobile she leaned close, "Sorry for being paranoid."

"It's okay," he said slipping an arm around her shoulders hugging her close. Hoping she would not expect sex.

"Let's go to bed," she said.

"Shag!" Pecker the parrot squawked.

"I think it associates the word bed with shag," he said with a glance behind them.

"Shag!" Squawked Dolly perched alongside Pecker.

"Shag!" Squawked Belle perched alongside Dolly.

"I think they know from our tone that we need sex," she mischievously grinned.

Disguising disinterest. A need to appear normal. Now not the time to show exhaustion. Jessica would spot any failure to do so with obvious conclusions. Bear Beddia support or not. Fortunately, as with everything he had a contingency. A packet of Viagra tucked beside his wallet. As they rose and headed for the bedroom the birds continued to squawk.

"Shag!"

"Shag!"

"Shag!"

"You really need to teach them another word," he told her closing the lounge door behind them.

She slapped his chest, "It's you who uses that word. You teach them."

CHAPTER EIGHTEEN

Power

Information is key to power. Never knowing enough about a rival, the motivation to discover more. Shaming them almost a hobby. That was the politics of the day although it might have always been could only be speculated. Today however, communications were instant and to be found in the living rooms of every home across the land. No one in the public eye could hope for privacy. Politicians were as much celebrities as entertainers. The only difference they generated contempt.

Being distrusted by a majority of the public is never a good starting point from which to accrue public support at general elections. For many years Rupert Streaker had watched with interest as potential candidates from successive governments lost trust followed soon after by defeat at elections. With only two years before the next general election time was not on his side, but he had made enormous gains with the public at the expense of losing support from his own Party. Acting as a centrist with a focus on improving infrastructure, health services and a complete restructure of central government primarily by relocating Parliament in the north at Blackburn together with the Monarchy he had achieved praised from many on the opposition benches. While rumblings of discontent occupied his own back benches. Surviving a leadership challenge before the next election appeared a serious possibility. One that looked harder to fend off by the day.

That rivals were aware of his predicament and likely enjoyed the circus behaving badly on the opposite benches only made matters worse. But no one had sympathy for a Prime Minister in opposition. Everyone wanted him destroyed no matter what good he might be providing the country. After all, it was the only way they themselves to grab the reins of power. The very reason for their being. Yet Rex Pounding the opposition leader was not inclined to damage Streaker if there was a way he might use him. The arrival of an anonymous A4 sized envelope with photographs and a short-handwritten message exposing something scandalous about Streaker that exceeded even his expectations took his breath away. However, now he had to establish that the allegation was true before a public statement could be made. His personal aide Penny Pulitzer could be relied upon to establish credibility. If true when to use it the next question.

As with all things timing is a priority. Get it right and you receive the best result. Being even slightly off and you may miss by a mile. Pounding knew that the timing of the latest scandal to reveal Streaker as an amoral individual would be best served at the next general election. For the moment he would keep it safely out of sight of the public and hoped whoever his anonymous anti-Streaker contributor was did the same.

Choosing to speak with his aide in the privacy of his office at Labour Headquarters he made sure they were first adequately supplied with coffee and biscuits. Besides the scandalous exposure he knew that she had news about the possibility of a backbench revolt by some hard-nosed Tories. Additionally, Lord Horny, although recovering from a serious accident appeared still able to cause discontentment among his peers. Who together with the backbenchers were in discussion about an attempted coup to topple Streaker?

Labour HQ at 105 Victoria Street Westminster had been occupied by Labour since the run up to the 2005 general election. A modern glassy look allowed the interior to be light and airy with a preference for modern furniture unlike the traditional 'old-world' furnishing found at Number 10.

Occupying a large office dominated by his desk Pounding sat contentedly behind it. The leather seat accommodating him creaking slightly with movement as Pulitzer used the seat opposite. While making herself comfortable he began to outline the reason she was there.

"What do you know about this possible coup. Who is orchestrating the moves against him?"

"No surprises there apart from the fact that he's still in hospital. Lord Horny is definitely one of the biggest antagonists. Closer to home, in the Commons it seems that Titus Oates is spinning all kinds of lies about where Streaker is taking the Tories. He really is doing our job for us," she chuckled. "You really can't better a backstabbing Tory."

"I take it some believe what he's saying?"

"Definitely, no matter how ridiculous it sounds. Streaker has some serious enemies within his Party who just want him gone."

"Do you have any idea who they're lining up to replace him?"

"Hugh Despenser. One of the richest men in the country."

Pounding frowned bothered by her answer. Despenser was a right-wing extremist likely to prove formidable as Prime Minister. Glorying in discrimination by agitating the indigenous population against immigration with accusations of criminality and the threat of impending job losses. He imagined Despenser intended sweeping changes in every arena relating to public services and support. A more callous leader he could not envisage. "Despenser is evil incarnate. If he gets in the entire country's in trouble. Are you certain they want him to take up the leadership? I mean he's more than just a bit extreme compared with Streaker. He'd even make Genghis Khan appear angelic."

"That's the name being bandied around the Commons," she gravely replied. Impossible not to share his concerns. "To be honest we'd be better off with Streaker at least he's been doing things that help the public. That certainly won't happen under Despenser."

"It appears that we need to keep with the Devil we know." He said reading her thoughts. "For the moment at least."

"Agreed," an expression of relief removing the grim expectation of the alternative. "Perhaps I should do a little research to bolster his supporters. Keep them from joining Despenser?"

"Dig up as much dirt on Despenser as you can find anything that hasn't been reported previously. It will have more value." He paused as if suddenly recalling something, "Also, see what you can find on Streaker's latest consultant Izzi Goeng. There's something about the man that raises my hackles."

"He's a super smooth player," she smiled. "Women adore him while men usually drip with envy. You're not feeling anything other rivals don't feel. You feel intimidated by him, it's natural." She had to admit Goeng was a damn handsome looking fella.

"Thanks for the psychology but it's more than that. No one is that good without leaving a sea of battered rivals in his wake. We need to know just how dirty he plays and if there's anyone chasing him."

"I'll do my best, but it might take a while if he's as clever as you think he is."

***

Jerome Shylocke was unaccustomed to receiving threats. Issuing them more his province. Today, was different. Today, after a brief conversation with Brian Belter Governor at the Bank of England he had discovered something unexpected about himself. He could still feel hurt. He wasn't immune from a very basic emotion. At least not by as much as he had believed himself to be. The top banker in the world could still feel emotional when it came to his standing in the world. He was meant to be above the emotional routines experienced by the millions on the lower rungs of life's ladder. Direct criticism a thing of the past or at least, that's what he assumed. The stark reality that someone considered him an equal and therefore vulnerable to attack, no matter how justified. Went beyond what he would permit.

After the call, his initial reaction had been to consider the threatening words sombrely. It was a reactionary phase one soon followed by anger and deeper reflection until he reached a calculation for retribution. To speak to him in such revealed nothing less than contempt for his most senior status. No one could be allowed to speak to him in such a way and get away with it. Not even the UK Prime Minister who Belter had been speaking on behalf.

However, the need to address a contemptuous elevated rival required planning. Fortunately, he knew the very people to pass on this outrage.

CHAPTER NINETEEN

Kate Allfores was in her office at Westminster when Izzi Goeng appeared in her doorway. Tall handsome with an enigmatic presence intended to cause any female to catch her breath. It would have been impossible for her reaction to appear any different and, given her history, he guessed she would welcome an invitation to work closely together.

"Kate Allfores, I'm Izzi Goeng. I believe Jonathon informed you I've been chosen to lead all major projects including yours."

"Yes," she replied, throat dry. Rising from her seat she moved around her desk offering a handshake. He accepted her hand in his own large encompassing fleshy palm. A strong grip enough to reveal physical power.

"I've been looking forward to meeting you. May I call you Kate?"

"Of course," she said recovering her hand. "What exactly will you need?"

"I need your timescales and what you hope to have achieved after you reach them. I need to ensure that what you're doing and when you're doing it seamlessly merges with all the other major projects going on. Additionally, I'll need an up-to-date spend assessment together with future projections of any additionally spending."

His dark eyes looking down from six feet five inches made her feel small, but in a nice way. Goeng had a presence that oozed confidence and an odd natural protection as if he could shield her from anything. "You said you were looking forward to meeting me, why is that?"

"I've read a lot about you. It's always interesting to meet someone unfairly castigated by the media."

"How do you know it was unfair?"

"Someone alleges you had sex with Streaker in a public place. He extricates himself without too much effort while you're thrown under the bus. The scenario is almost a cliché."

"You sound as if you don't believe the Prime Minister," she replied.

"Let's say I've been around long enough to know who pulls the strings when required."

"Enough said about him," she smiled. Tell me how you got the job of project co-ordinator when no one else had even heard of it until you showed up."

"Rupert made me an offer I couldn't refuse. That's it really."

"At least you have the credentials to prove you're capable of doing the job."

"Meaning?"

"Very few of our peers are qualified to run a bath let alone a major project. The old boys network still guarantees a huge salary for chums of the Prime Minister whether they're up to the job or not."

"You sound like a disgruntled member of the public."

"Cronyism is rife. I've had to work my butt off to do as well as I have done," she caught his grin. "Yes literally."

"Clearly it's worth it because you're here," he smirked. "I'm glad. I can usually tell whether I'm going to get along with someone. You tick all the right boxes."

"Should I feel lucky?"

"Not lucky. Happy that you have a new ally. One that won't let you down."

"We only just met Izzi and although I don't deny you've captured my interest that doesn't mean we're tying the knot any time soon."

"I don't waste time when I meet someone who interests me. We should meet tonight for dinner. I could collect you at seven thirty."

"You could if I agreed, but we only just met and….."

"Eight then, give you a little more time to get yourself ready for a wonderful evening."

"You really don't take no for an answer," she replied, struggling to hide the fact that she was intrigued. "You realize we haven't talked about the project enough."

"You've an idea what I need. Whatever you send I'm sure will prove sufficiently comprehensive. If not it will give me an excuse to pay you another visit. Now what do you say?"

She moved slowly around the desk opened a drawer and lifted out a business card to hand him. "Eight it is."

After he had gone leaving her alone she dropped into a chair uncertain whether she was dreaming.

At around five that afternoon Shylocke called for a progress report from the man hired to bring down Streaker. "Well?"

Never one for small chat with underlings he patiently waited three seconds for the response he wanted to hear. "I'm in."

"Good. What about Kate Allfores?"

"I'm meeting her tonight. By tomorrow I should have all we need to expose Streaker as a liar. His Party will be unable to allow him to continue. "

"And his wife?"

"No guarantees but my understanding is that she'll want blood. She believes their relationship is built on honesty. When this gets out she'll be humiliated. Never known a woman yet who enjoys that kind of embarrassment."

"Are you sure this matter will be sufficient to destroy him?"

"The way things are at the moment he's not the Party favourite. The knives are already out. This will definitely be enough."

"Make sure it happens if you want to be paid Coeng!"

"It will and I do," he said as Shylocke abruptly ended the call. Slipping the mobile into a jacket pocket while striding towards the parliament buildings at Westminster. Confident that the £5 million pounds he was to be paid after Streaker was toppled could be considered as banked.

The  End

Printed in Great Britain
by Amazon

60748966R00099